William P. Robertson [signature]

ATTACK IN THE ALLEGHENIES

by

William P. Robertson & David Rimer

All rights reserved. No part of this book shall be reproduced or transmitted in any form or by any means, electronic, mechanical, magnetic, photographic including photocopying, recording or by any information storage and retrieval system, without prior written permission of the publisher. No patent liability is assumed with respect to the use of the information contained herein. Although every precaution has been taken in the preparation of this book, the publisher and author assume no responsibility for errors or omissions. Neither is any liability assumed for damages resulting from the use of the information contained herein.

Copyright © 2010 by William P. Robertson & David Rimer

ISBN 0-7414-5897-7

Printed in the United States of America

This is a work of fiction. Names, characters, places, and incidents either are the product of the author's imagination or are used fictitiously. Any resemblance to actual events or locales or persons, living or dead, is entirely coincidental.

Published October 2010

INFINITY PUBLISHING
1094 New DeHaven Street, Suite 100
West Conshohocken, PA 19428-2713
Toll-free (877) BUY BOOK
Local Phone (610) 941-9999
Fax (610) 941-9959
Info@buybooksontheweb.com
www.buybooksontheweb.com

CONTENTS

1. A TOUGH HUNT 1
2. TRAPS 7
3. HEADIN' DOWNRIVER 13
4. THE ESCAPE 19
5. KIT-HAN-NE 25
6. SON OR PRISONER? 31
7. THE FRENCH COME TO CALL 38
8. BLACK FISH 44
9. MORE GAMES 51
10. THE RAIDERS RETURN 56
11. HIDE AND SEEK 64
12. A COLD RIVER RIDE 71
13. A JOYFUL REUNION 77
14. SPRING AT LAST 86
15. BURIAL RITES 91
16. MORE DANGER 97
17. THE BLAZE 103
18. ANOTHER LONG JOURNEY 111
19. FORT GRANVILLE 117
20. THE DEVIL TO PAY 127
21. ATTACK ON KIT-HAN-NE 135
22. THE RETREAT 145
23. GIFTS 153

BIBLIOGRAPHY 160

Reenactor Brett Meoisko portrays a warrior of the Delaware nation that spread terror across the frontier of Pennsylvania after Braddock's defeat on July 9, 1755.

ACKNOWLEDGMENTS

The authors would like to thank the following French & Indian War reenactors for their participation in this project: Arron Oliphant, British regular; Ben Delaney, Dennis McKibben, George Standing Elk, Robert Stray Wolf, Cliff Two Hawks, Bill Two Bears Graham, Greg Rearick, Joe Rearick, Brett Meoisko, Rich Serafin, Jon Miller, Aaron Bosnick, Jim Edwards, Joe Miranda, James Blake (Delaware and Shawnee warriors); Corey Taylor, Marc Jackson (Iroquois braves); Alex Efremenko (French militien); Ron Peterson, Larry Fox, Barry Sagar (Ohio Company Rangers); Cynthia Stillman (captive white girl); the Augusta Regiment (Pennsylvania provincial troops w/ Mike Slease unit leader) & Bob Houben (free trapper).

A special thanks goes out to Dale Luthringer of Cook Forest State Park, Cooksburg, PA, where many of the photos were taken during their French & Indian War reenactment. Thanks also to historian, Greg Rearick, who provided valuable information about Kit-Han-Ne and the black fish game.

Finally, a tip of the hat to David Cox, who painted the cover of <u>Attack in the Alleghenies</u>. David is a prize-winning freelance artist from Bradford, PA, and an accomplished teacher of art and martial arts. He also illustrated William P. Robertson's poetry collections <u>1066</u>, <u>Hearse Verse</u>, and <u>The Illustrated Book of Ancient, Medieval & Fantasy Battle Verse</u> and did the cover art for <u>Ambush in the Alleghenies</u>.

The majority of the photos in this book were taken by William P. Robertson. He also created the Alleghenies Circa 1755 map and the Kit-Han-

Ne map on his computer. The latter was based upon that drawn for Lt. Colonel John Armstrong by John Baker. Baker escaped the Indians at Kittanning and knew the layout of the village.

Robertson's author photo was shot by Larry Fox. David Rimer's author photo was taken by his wife, Marcia. Other photos were provided by Greg Rearick of Clarion, PA, and Randy Quinn of Kittanning, PA. The back cover photo of Ben Delaney was shot by Randy Quinn, as well. Gary T. Gibson contributed the photo of Indians in canoes. Gary is the photographer/owner of The Clarion River Picture Company, Vandergrift, PA. Phone him at 724-567-1939. The Long Art Company did the front cover photography. Contact Francie Long at longartphoto.com.

Greg Rearick and Bill Two Bears Graham stand outside a Delaware-style bark hut they built for the Cook Forest 2007 French & Indian War reenactment.

COOK FOREST AND CUSTALOGA TOWN: BATTLES PROVIDE AUTHENTIC THRILLS

The Cook Forest and Custaloga Town French and Indian War encampments, held respectively the second and third weekends in June, offer reenactors and the public alike a unique opportunity to experience forest battles as they were fought in Western Pennsylvania during the colonial period of the 1750's. Cook Forest, located south of Marionville on Route 66, and Custaloga Town, the site of an old Indian Village just north of Franklin off Route 322, still provide the same forest setting that sheltered the original combatants over 200 years ago.

The 2009 Cook Forest event featured an all-out assault by French forces against a makeshift log fort defended by a Scotch and British unit armed with muskets and two small cannon. The French and their Indian allies swept down a heavily wooded hill to surround the beleaguered Brits, who fired furiously to hold off their shrieking assailants. The black powder guns soon created a heavy pall of smoke that masked the movements of the attacking force. Finally, the firepower of the British artillery held sway, and the white-clad contingent of French retreated into the forest.

The Custaloga Town battles were more on the order of skirmishes than the Cook Forest affair. In the morning fight, the colonial rangers ambushed the French and Indians as they attacked a small force of British regulars in their bright red coats. The British were actually the bait used to draw their opponents into the trap. The rangers stayed concealed in the bushy woods until the enemy drew even with them and then poured deadly fire into the French right flank. The volley left King Louis' men reeling, and they were forced to scatter into the forest beyond.

The afternoon battle turned the tables on the British, who attempted to attack the French camp. As the Brits advanced through the woods, they were spotted by Indian scouts, and all surprise was lost. The French immediately formed into a solid rank and fired one effective volley after another into the redcoats and colonial rangers. The Indians, meanwhile, worked their way around the faltering enemy's line and forced them to withdraw, leaving many dead and wounded littering the ground behind them. These downed soldiers brought shrieks of delight from the Native Americans, for soon there would be many scalps hanging from their lodge poles.

Of course, safety first is the order of the day for these modern reenactments. No filled powder horns are allowed on the field because they could become bombs in the hands of green participants. Instead, paper cartridges filled with exact charges of black powder are used to load the muskets. When the muskets are discharged in battle, all guns are fired well over the heads of the opposing army to protect their soldiers from the force of the muzzle blasts. Also, no ramrods are allowed for fear that an excited combatant might leave one in his gun and shoot it accidentally like an arrow. In addition, before each battle, all muskets are inspected to insure they're in proper working order.

Despite these safety restrictions, the soldiers and Indians are dressed in such detailed, authentic garb that they provide a scintillating experience for gawking spectators. The Indian warriors are especially scary with their faces painted and tattooed. When the howling Delaware and Shawnees come bursting out of the woods, even experienced soldiers of many reenactment campaigns pull their tricorns tighter on their heads to secure their topknots!

Above, Arron Oliphant portrays a British soldier.

INTRODUCTION

Following General Edward Braddock's defeat on July 9, 1755, near Fort Duquesne, the British abandoned the Pennsylvania frontier. This allowed an onslaught of Indian war parties to wreak havoc upon the region. The Delaware now joined the French and Shawnees and began a reign of terror, burning out settlers at a fearful rate west of the Susquehanna River. The massacres began at Penn's Creek where hostiles killed, scalped, or captured all 25 inhabitants. Other atrocities soon followed, including the brutal raids into the Big and Little Coves just west of the Kittatinny Mountains. The slaying of Moravian missionaries at Gnadenhuetten in Carbon County showed just how vulnerable Pennsylvania had become to the Indian menace.

Finally, on November 26, 1755, the Pennsylvania Assembly, dominated by pacifist Quakers, was persuaded by Governor Robert Morris and a flood of petitions from terrified citizens to fund a string of forts. These forts stretched along the Blue Mountains from the Delaware River to the Maryland line and acted as a chain of defense near important mountain passes. But even such strongholds, manned by paid militia, did little to quell the ongoing massacres. It wasn't until after a howling band of Delaware burned Fort Granville on July 30, 1756, that Lieutenant Colonel John Armstrong of the Pennsylvania Second Battalion convinced the leaders of the province to take the fight to the Indians and attack Kit-Han-Ne.

THE ALLEGHENIES CIRCA 1755

CHAPTER ONE: A TOUGH HUNT

Lightnin' Jack Hawkins peered through the trees at the line of hunters slinking along noiselessly to his right. His companions were dressed in buckskins and blended in perfectly with the shadowy forest that engulfed them. Stretched out at thirty yard intervals, they reminded Jack of a skirmish line of Braddock's advanced scouts. A scowl passed over the young woodsman's tanned face as he remembered the terrible slaughter the British general had led them into near Fort Duquesne. Now, the whole frontier was filled with howling hostiles thirsting for his scalp because of that redcoat's pride and incompetence. Most of the life-sustaining game had disappeared, too, and a pervading sense of doom spread through the vast wilderness of the Alleghenies.

It was a frosty fall morning, and Jack took extra care not to crunch the frozen leaves underfoot. Only orange and yellow foliage remained, while the naked oaks groaned with every cold gust of wind. Like all good hunters, Hawkins kept that wind in his face, so the creatures he stalked couldn't catch his scent. His moccasins moved with a whisper until he came to a thicket where the chickadees and nuthatches flitted in great profusion. The busy birds were sating their appetites on beechnuts, and Jack figured deer and turkeys could be feeding here, too.

Lightnin' signaled for his friends to halt. Then, he scanned the curtain of rattling beech leaves with his quick, dark eyes. He also needed to catch his breath because he'd been sneaking along with hushed anticipation since dawn. There'd been no meat for over a week. The gnawing in Hawkins' belly had added a sense of urgency to this hunt.

Jack inhaled a frosty draught of air into his lungs and blew it slowly out his flared nostrils. Afterward, he turned to check on his mates. Like him, they had paused behind tree trunks to conceal their presence. Nearest to Hawkins was the sour Scot, Alexander MacDonald, whose face was constantly twisted in a sardonic sneer. Mac's wool tam was pulled low over his forehead to just above his heavy roan eyebrows. He clutched his long rifle in his ruddy hands and twitched nervously as if a dangerous savage lurked behind every bush.

Thirty yards beyond MacDonald crouched Bearbite Bob Winslow. The old hunter tugged at his white, chest-length beard and then sniffed the wind like a predatory beast. He knew the scent of every creature that roamed these woods, and Jack hoped his grizzled pal would sniff out a buck or even a tough old bear.

The sun burst suddenly from a break in the October clouds, and Lightnin' squinted until he located Will Cutler, who was farthest from him. He could just make out the flax-colored mop of hair that stuck out from beneath the lad's coonskin cap. Even at a distance of ninety yards, Cutler's pose exuded a confidence only known by those in their teens. Jack's face split into a wide grin as he muttered to himself, "Will's gonna need every ounce o' that pluck married to the hellcat princess he hooked up with."

Hawkins surveyed the brush one last time. Then, he took a false step that snapped a fallen branch like the crack of a musket. The noise no sooner washed into the beech when a huge doe leaped up from its bed only a few yards from where Jack stood cursing his clumsiness. The hunter lurched backward in surprise, while the spooked deer lunged through the trees, pumping its legs and raising its white tail in alarm.

The doe blew by Mac before he could cock his rifle, and snorting with fear, bounded toward Bearbite Bob. With shaky hands, Bob aimed his flintlock at the streaking deer, yanked the trigger, and shot clean over the beast's back. The blast pushed the doe into high gear, and it dashed to trample Will, who stood blocking its escape. The lad held his ground until the last possible instant before dodging behind a huge oak. The deer only missed him by inches as it bolted past.

Cutler cocked his long rifle and raised it to his shoulder. He swung the barrel to follow the panicked beast's flight and coolly discharged his weapon as the doe raced to the edge of an adjacent hillside. Just before the deer disappeared down the slope, it looked as though a huge hand slammed it unmoving to the ground.

Will rushed to collect his kill with a victory yelp issuing from his lips. When his friends joined him in his celebration, they were amazed to find the lad had hit the doe where its head connected to its neck, killing it instantly.

"Waugh!" cried Hawkins, bending to examine the fallen animal. "That was the best runnin' shot I ever seen. How did ya do that, Big Cat?"

"Just swung with her is all," explained Will. "And kept my head."

"Not like you, Lightnin'," needled Winslow. "When that doe leaped up, ya shied away from her like a scared girl. It's a wonder ya didn't squeal, too."

"'Least I didn't burn powder an' miss!"

"Aye, Bob, ye pulled that shot like a greenhorn," jeered MacDonald.

"Then, why didn't you blast the doe?" challenged Bearbite. "Has all that soft livin' with the Iroquois made ya too weak ta pull back yer hammer?"

"That's enough," chided Cutler. "Don't you know we have to give thanks for this deer? Be quiet while I pray."

"The lad's right," replied Mac with a sheepish grin. "I'm sorry. Go ahead."

"Oh, Great Spirit, please accept our thankfulness for this fine creature who gave her life so we may survive. We will use her well."

Will had barely finished his prayer when Jack knelt to slit open the deer's belly. Fishing inside the chest cavity, he jerked free the warm liver and cut it in chunks that he passed to the other ravenous hunters. As he feasted on delicious raw flesh, he said, "Sure glad ya come along on this hunt, Will, er all we'd have ta show fer it would be wore-out moccasins an' draggin' rears."

"What made ya change yer mind 'bout joinin' us?" asked Bearbite. "If I had a sweet, young flower at Ishua Town, I'd be back there sniffin' her petals instead o' trampin' the woods with these boys."

"Oh, Bright Star's pretty all right," sighed Will, "but some nights you might as well try hugging a porcupine."

"Then, ya don't know if you're on foot er horseback when it comes to squaws," chortled Bearbite.

"Hey, I grew up with six sisters, and they weren't cold as the ashes of a day old fire! I want a houseful of kids, but Bright Star will have none of it. I thought Bear clan women were supposed to be fond of children and babies."

"Aye, they're also known to forgive but never forget. I'd take it slow with her if it be me," advised Alex. "Ye still have your whole life to raise up a family."

"But this wilderness has a way of crushing the life out of everything it touches," mourned Cutler. "No one stays young here very long. Lightnin', how do you think I should handle Bright Star?"

"I wouldn't have got tangled up with her to begin with. A mountain man's like a strong wind. He ain't supposed to be penned up by no woman.

I got an itch inside me that don't let me rest. All I want out o' life is ta see what's over the next ridge an' hunt er trap it."

"I'm right with ya," cackled Winslow. "Bear Woman is fine fer now, but by spring I want to be harvestin' some new beaver."

"Speakin' o' beaver, I best go check our traps ag'in. Then, I won't have to listen to all this fool talk 'bout squaws."

"Do ye want some company?" muttered Mac. "Now that the Delaware have joined the Frenchies, it may not be safe a wanderin' off on your own."

"Hell no!" rumbled Lightnin' with an annoyed nod of his head. "Does the wind need someone taggin' along when it shakes the trees er leaps from hill to hill?"

"Aren't you at least going to stay for dinner?" asked Big Cat while he cut steaks from a skinned hindquarter of the doe.

"If I stays any longer, it'll be dark before I git back to Ishua Town. See ya at the village."

"Them trapped beaver will keep another day," reminded Bob. "Why don't ya stick around, an' we'll go tomorrow mornin' to collect our plews?"

"No, I'm mighty restless. A walk to that pond will do me an' Little Lightnin' a lot o' good," grunted Hawkins, giving his long rifle a loving pat.

"Then, watch yer topknot."

"An' watch yourn."

CHAPTER TWO: TRAPS

Lightnin' Jack felt strangely agitated as he followed a dim trail across a rocky highland. There was something in the air today that he couldn't put his finger on, and the rangy woodsman shuddered as he watched a pair of turkey vultures circle ominously overhead. He finally arrived at the edge of a narrow, wooded valley. Here, he plunged down a gravel bank and slid all the way to the valley bottom in an avalanche of dirt and fine stones.

Hawkins stopped inches from a gurgling brook. After dusting himself off, he trotted urgently downstream. He continued to lope along with his long rifle tucked under his right arm until he reached a wide beaver dam stretching across a flooded meadow.

Creeping along the margins of the dam, Jack checked for tree cuttings, bank burrows, and other signs of recent beaver activity. When he found not even a freshly gnawed hunk of tree bark, his face dissolved into a dismal frown. Slipping off his moccasins, he waded knee-deep into the icy water toward a pole jutting out of the pond. The trap positioned beneath the pole had not been sprung, so Hawkins waded along shore to visit his other sets.

Disappointment reflected from Jack's eyes when he stomped empty-handed up the soggy bank. As he pulled on his moccasins, he growled aloud, "Should be out explorin' new woods instead o' trappin' on used-up Iroquois' land. Bein' cooped up in Ishua Town has dulled my edge!"

In a fury, Hawkins reentered the forest and struck a well-traveled trail that he knew led back to the Allegheny. With his sinewy legs eating up the ground beneath him, he strode along vaguely noting the tracks of coons, deer, and wolves that had trod the path before him. Man-tracks were there, too, and Lightnin' suddenly remembered the reports of Delaware war parties that runners brought daily to Ishua Town.

"Why couldn't the Injuns have stirred up their bloodlust after me an' the boys went trappin' fer the winter?" muttered Jack as he entered a murky wood. "Now, we's out o' work, an' what are--"

Hawkins' second question was interrupted by a teeth-rattling blow. Immediately after, he was slammed to ground by an enormous weight that knocked his rifle from his grasp. For several moments he lay senseless, pinned beneath an undetermined enemy. When the blackness finally receded from his vision, an excruciating pain caused him to faint again. It wasn't until the cobwebs finally lifted from his brain that he found himself the victim of a deadfall trap.

For the longest time Jack lay very still. Finally, he wiggled the fingers of his right hand and then stretched his legs to check their range of motion. His left arm, though, was pinned under the fallen log. Whenever he tried to tug it loose, he was zapped by a jolt of nerve lightning.

Sweat poured down Hawkins' forehead in a blinding flood. Using his free hand, he mopped away the perspiration and then wrapped his body around the log that restrained him. In one adrenaline-charged motion, he rolled madly to his right until he freed his crushed limb. The log ground over his arm in the process, and a yelp sprang of its own accord from Jack's throat.

Somehow, the hunter wobbled to his feet and staggered up the shadowy path. Every step caused him horrible pain until he stopped suddenly to vomit. He continued to stumble along before going into shock. His vision was so blurred that he floundered past the well-marked side trail leading to Ishua Town.

Hawkins tottered absently along to the west until darkness engulfed him. It was a moonless night, and the October chill pushed the ache in his injured arm to an unbearable level. His teeth chattered uncontrollably, too, as the cold penetrated his body.

Soon, Jack's legs grew so numb that he thought he was walking in shackles. Still, he continued to grope his way along like a prisoner in an obscure maze. Several times he blundered into the brush to have his face raked with pointy branches. After another mile of agony, every joint, tendon, and muscle twitched in protest with each half-step he managed.

Hawkins was about to collapse in a quivering heap when he lurched around a bend and saw a flickering campfire not a hundred yards down the umbra-ridden trail. With his last spurt of energy, Lightnin' tottered ahead pleading, "Help! Help! Help me!"

When no one answered his imploring cries, Jack feared he'd stumbled on savages. It was only upon reaching the circle of firelight that he learned of which breed. There, leering at him from their campfire, were the rum selling vermin he and his buddies had driven from Ishua Town. Their fat faces twisted into leers as they swilled liquor and contemplated the vulnerable state of their uninvited guest. When the pair snatched up hatchets and sprang to their feet, Hawkins again lapsed into unconsciousness.

Jack felt foul-smelling liquid splatter on his face. He jerked awake to find the traders dancing around him like drunken bears. The ruffians were dressed in filthy smocks and weather-stained tricorns. Their calf-length boots reeked of horse manure and their clothing of human sweat. Their cheeks were covered with three days' pig stubble. Their lips were stained by chewing tobacco. Each time they stopped their gyrating, they sprayed Lightnin' with another barrage of tobacco spit.

Hawkins tried to rise and defend himself, but the pain in his arm buckled him back to his haunches. It was then that the stoutest scoundrel slurred to his companion, "Hey, Randall, ain't this one of the knaves who muddied the water for us with the Iroquois?"

"Sure is, Rupert," sniggered the other barrel-chested ruffian. "An' look. The ungrateful cur don't like the shower we's givin' 'im."

"Then, maybe he'll take to the soles of our boots!"

"Aye, tit for tat, I always say!"

"That's it, governor, we'll show him the latest steps, straight from London. It's all the rage among the genteel class, ya know."

Randall immediately placed his hands on his hips and broke into a lively jig more suitable to an Irish tavern than an English palace. Bouncing repeatedly from heel to toe, he closed upon the prostrate Hawkins and began booting him viciously each time his toe clicked forward. After delivering a non-stop, two-minute flurry of kicks, he bowed to his crony and motioned for him to pick up the dance.

"It appears ta me," snarled Rupert, "that this chap prefers the heel to the toe. I'll show ya."

The burly trader still had a sore knee from Will Cutler smacking it with a musket butt, so he simply took to kicking Jack with his one good leg. By then, Hawkins had curled up in a ball with only his back exposed to the terrible drubbing. The punishment continued until hobbled horses outside the firelight began to snort nervously.

Randall took another draught of liquor. As he pulled his partner away from Lightnin', he cackled, "Them animals got more sense than us. You best stop before ya do 'im some real harm."

"Ah-h-h! You're ruinin' all my fun," protested Rupert. "Come on. Let's see how he takes to hatchet throwin'."

"You don't want to ruin the merchandise, do ya? The Delaware won't give us beans if ya kill 'im. Hey, no wonder he didn't put up a fight. He's got a busted wing."

"Well, you're the horse doctor. You can set that arm an' fix 'im up with a proper sling."

"I wonder why the wretch is unarmed?"

"Musta lost his rifle wanderin' around in the dark," grunted Rupert. "Too bad he didn't break his neck!"

"Why don't we backtrack an' find his gun? That'd bring us prime plews from the Injuns, too."

"No, we don't wanna get close to Ishua Town just yet."

"But we have to go back an' slit his young friend's throat, don't we?" hissed Randall.

"No, we'll bide our time, we will," insisted the other rogue, whacking his hatchet in the ground inches from Jack's quivering neck.

"I git it. We'll hit 'im when he least expects it. Hack off his ears. Then, his nose."

"Injun-style torture, slow an' painful."

"First, we need ta sell this trapper at Kit-Han-Ne," reminded Randall.

"Good thing we got more rum cached downstream. After them Delaware git drunk, they'll flay every inch o' skin off 'im!"

CHAPTER THREE: HEADIN' DOWNRIVER

When Hawkins started awake the next morning, he was tied upright on a moving horse. Although his arm still throbbed, it was now bound in a sling. That made the pounding of the beast's hooves beneath him at least bearable. Staring ahead, he found himself in the midst of a train of horses that splashed down a trail-side stream. Two of the mounts carried trade goods, while the lead mare strained beneath the weight of a burly brute of a man. Lightnin' could hear another horse kicking up water behind him.

Jack glanced quizzically about until a raspy voice growled from the rear, "Ya didn't think we'd leave tracks for your friends to follow? Every trader knows better 'n that!"

Hawkins turned to face the villain of his recent nightmare. A twinge emanated from his bruised back as a cascade of heavy kicks flooded through his memory. Finally, he quipped, "An' here I thought this was how you rascals bathed an' washed yer duds. I bet this is the closest ya been ta water since yer mama took the lye soap to ya."

Rupert snatched a furled whip from around his saddle horn and snapped it inches from Jack's ear. "Shut yer face," he snarled. "Us Millers will fling the insults from now on."

"That's right!" seconded his brother Randall from the lead horse. "Show some respect, er we'll bust yer other arm."

The pack train continued to splash through the creek until it came to a foaming waterfall. Here, Randall guided his mount back onto the trail where he found a multitude of fresh moccasin tracks. Pointing them out to Rupert, he grunted, "Looks like we's close to Buck Tooth. Better dismount an' take ta the woods. Help our prisoner git down. Don't want 'im stickin' outta the brush when we skirt them Iroquois."

Pushing off into a beech thicket, the pack train crept slowly along with the brothers slipping from animal to animal to quiet them when they snorted. Just off to the left they could hear the soft humming of squaws as they prepared their evening meals. Children's laughter and the barking of dogs also marked the boundaries of the Indian village.

When the chorus of Iroquois voices was well behind them, the Millers returned to the trail and pressed along until dark. The rush of the Allegheny River now accompanied them, and they could just see the moonlight glisten from the dark water. Finally, Randall exhaled a mighty yawn and muttered, "We best stop for the night before our horses git too tired to carry us tomorrow."

"Ain't ya worried 'bout me?" scolded Hawkins. "If I fall an' bust my noggin', I won't be worth nothin' in trade."

"Then, we'll dump ya in the river," promised Rupert, "an' good riddance!"

The Millers yanked Jack from the saddle and tied him rudely against a tree. Then, they unloaded the heavy packs and saddles from their mounts and carefully rubbed down the weary animals' legs and flanks. After brushing the mares' manes, they gave them handfuls of oats from an open saddlebag.

"Hey, when do I git fed?" grumbled Lightnin'. "My belly's touchin' my backbone."

"Ya don't!" exclaimed Randall, taking a pull from a flask he produced from a deerskin pouch. "We's outta flour, an' I'm too tired to go fishin'."

"How 'bout a slug o' that rotgut?"

"Sorry," grunted Rupert. "We don't give liquor to our animals."

Randall and Rupert led their pack train downriver for three more days. Twice, they hid in the brush to avoid Iroquois hunting parties and twice more to keep Indian runners from spotting them. Several times a day they stopped to water their horses or fish in the Allegheny. Meals now consisted of raw or cooked catfish, depending upon if it were safe to build a small fire. After slipping past the town of Shinango on a foggy morning, the Miller brothers exchanged wide grins and gave Jack the same look they'd have bestowed on a stack of silver coins.

Later that afternoon, Randall halted his mount beside a rotted elm that leaned precariously over the trail. Rupert immediately galloped to his side, and they dismounted to lumber up a dark ravine. They reappeared soon after carrying a keg of rum between them. Carefully, they tied the keg to the side of their tallest horse and chuckled gleefully as though very pleased with themselves.

"You boys plannin' to drink that rum er sell it?" cracked Lightnin'. "Either way you'll profit from it."

"Shut up, or we'll slice off that glib tongue," threatened Rupert.

"An' have somethin' besides fish to roast," snarled his brother.

Just before dusk, the party topped an incline in the trail and saw smoke rising from chimneys where a stream from the north merged with the Allegheny. "There's Venango just ahead!" yelped Randall. "The Frenchies will be mighty glad to see the cargo we's haulin'."

"I thought them boys was supplied with their own 'cargo,' the way they pass it out to the Injuns," croaked Lightnin'.

"A drunk Delaware makes a better customer," sneered Rupert. "Any white man knows that."

"An' a thief's a thief no matter if ya call 'im a robber er a highwayman," muttered Jack under his breath.

The pack train picked up speed as it headed down the slope toward the village. Nervously, Jack surveyed the French stockade that was flanked by a jumble of log houses and Indian wigwams. A flock of barefoot children rushed toward them when they emerged from the woods. The youngsters' high-pitched cries reminded Hawkins of blue jays as they fluttered excitedly around the visitors.

Soon, the party was met by a patrol of soldiers dressed in white uniform coats and pants. A flicker of recognition passed through the eyes of the lieutenant in charge, and he said in broken English, "So ze Millers grow tired of Iroquois hospitality? Who is it you have weeth you tied up like ze Christmas package? Is he a gift for Captain Joncaire? Canada has need of English dogs to slave in our fields. If he trap illegally, we send him to Montreal for trial, no?"

"No, no! This man's in business with us," lied Randall, flashing an oily smile. "His horse threw 'im, an' we tied him in the saddle to keep 'im safe. See. I set his broken arm. Would I do that for any damn trapper?"

"I guess not," replied the pale officer, coughing into his hand, "but somehow this fellow looks familiar."

"Sure, you saw 'im with us on our way upriver. Don't ya remember?" asked Rupert.

"No, that's not it. Oh, well, no matter. You're always welcome in Venango when you bring news of ze Iroquois or Anglais. Come along. I will put you up in ze barracks."

Jack gulped hard when he heard their destination. The last time he visited here with Mac, they had knocked out sentries, banged holes in the bottom of a row of canoes, and barely escaped with their topknots. With his free hand, he plucked the coonskin cap from his head and hoped a five-day stubble would hide his identity from the inevitable scrutiny of Joncaire.

As luck would have it, Randall said just before they reached the French fort, "Ya know, lieutenant, it might be best if we camp out here on the beach. We stink powerful bad from our horses, an' I know how your captain hates that. If ya got some flour an' dried beans to trade for a little rum, we'd be most grateful."

"Consider it done," replied the officer, choking back a sneeze. "I will personally see to it."

As the soldiers marched back into the stockade, Randall led his party down to the river's edge where they unloaded their supplies and trading goods next to a long dugout canoe that sat separate from the other boats. "You rest here," he said to his brother, "an' I'll board our horses at the stable. We best leave as soon possible."

"Before we gits our flour an' beans?" bemoaned Rupert.

"No, before they remember I'm Lightnin' Jack Hawkins!" exclaimed the trapper, cradling his busted arm. "Then, we'll all rot in a Montreal jail!"

CHAPTER FOUR: THE ESCAPE

Randall had barely returned from the stable when the French lieutenant and two privates came hustling down the beach. The enlisted men carted heavy sacks of flour and beans, while the officer clutched three tankards in his pale hand. After the soldiers had stowed the supplies in Randall's canoe, he had no choice but to tap the rum keg. In response, the soldiers saluted Miller with mock sincerity. Then, they began swilling large quantities of the potent liquor.

The more the French drank, however, the more suspicious they became of Jack. Several times the lieutenant stared long in his face, while the enlisted men conferred together after gesturing toward Hawkins. Fearing the soldiers might recognize Lightnin' at any moment, Randall began stowing their belongings into the big dugout canoe whenever the drunks had their backs to him. Even the less than ambitious Rupert was nervous and slinked off to help his brother until everything but the keg was safely aboard.

Just as darkness was about to fall, the lieutenant staggered to his feet and blared to Jack, "I know I've seen you before, monsieur. I'm sure it was here. At ze fort. Men, build a fire, so I can have a better look at him."

"That ain't necessary," sputtered Randall with mock indignation. "Didn't I already vouch for this man? If that's how ya treat us after sharin' our hospitality, it's time we head downriver."

"But ze rapids. Aren't you afraid in the failing light?"

"No, we've shot 'em a hundred times," assured the trader, pulling Jack to his feet. "We got a long trip ahead. Keep the rum as a token of our friendship. See ya next time."

"B-B-But, Monsieur Miller, don't you have anything to tell us about ze Iroquois?"

"They ain't doin' nothin' but huntin' an' playin' lacrosse," replied Randall, backing toward the Allegheny. "Gotta go."

Rupert was already squatting in the stern of the canoe. As soon as his brother and Hawkins were seated, he propelled them into the current. Randall immediately joined in the paddling, and their craft shot away from the riverbank and the gawking soldiers.

In the distance Lightnin' could hear a steady roar, and fear visited his brow as he recollected his last hurried exit from Venango. He barely had time to gulp in dismay when the dugout shot headlong down a chute of rapids that defined the meaning of whitewater. His two companions, however, remained unfazed by their plight and coolly guided the canoe through a maze of sharp rocks and hissing flux. Somehow, they avoided the wreck of a log raft and then mightily worked their paddles to steer clear of a whirlpool. The flood spit them out into a deep run just as the final glint of dusk faded from the forest.

The traders beached their dugout and tottered ashore. They were too exhausted to build a fire, so they dragged Jack out of the canoe and tied him up the best they could in the dark. When Hawkins didn't resist or talk back, the Millers paid him no further mind. Wrapping themselves in their blankets, they instantly sank into a deep slumber.

Randall didn't regain consciousness until the squawking of grackles roused him well past sunrise. Popping open his bloodshot pig eyes, he stared toward the river and then shifted his gaze to check on Jack. In the next instant he scrambled to his feet and roared, "Git up, Rupert! Git up! Our damn prisoner's wiggled outta his ropes. He's gone!"

"Gone?" croaked his brother, exhaling a foul-smelling yawn. "He couldn't have got far."

"Git up! Hawkins is a woodsman. He knows every inch of these here mountains. We better ketch him quick, or we won't ketch 'im at all!"

The Miller brothers stomped off into the woods growling a string of filthy curses. They followed Lightnin's dim tracks through a frosty glen bursting with mushrooms. Their quarry had breakfasted there as evident by the pawed ground. Rupert and Randall helped themselves, too, before plunging into a swampy bottomland.

Jack's footprints were gobbled up by the marsh, but that didn't prevent Randall from tracking him by way of bent reeds. He forged eagerly ahead with his brother on his heels expecting any moment to run down their prey. Hawkins must have known they were closing in because suddenly his sign veered off into the worst part of the bog. Now, each time the Millers took a step, it was accompanied by a telltale sucking sound as they sank calf-deep into the black muck. No matter if they went fast or slow, a loud splashing followed them.

The Millers continued to slog on until they came to a patch of quicksand that appeared in the midst of the reeds. The brothers almost knocked each other down while avoiding the quagmire. Unfortunately, Jack hadn't been that lucky. He was trapped armpit-deep in the slop and dared not move for fear of sinking farther.

"Ya ain't so fast after all, are ya, Lightnin'?" jeered Rupert.

"Don't swim worth a lick, neither," mocked Randall.

"I reckon not," gulped Hawkins. "Are ya gonna help me, er what?"

"I think we should let him sink up to his nose first," suggested Rupert. "For runnin' away."

"Naw, that'd be cuttin' her too close," replied his brother. "The Injuns won't give us nothin' for a drown swamp rat."

While Rupert continued to insult Jack, Randall sloshed to a nearby island. Pulling a deadly-looking knife from its sheath, he hacked a stout branch from a hickory tree. Wading back to his brother's side, he extended the limb to Hawkins, who grabbed it with his good hand. Jack was stuck too deep for Randall to pull him out, so Rupert wrapped his arms around his brother's waist and both men began splashing backward. By combining their weight and power, they steadily dragged Hawkins to safety.

Once Lightnin' was on dry land, Rupert gave him a nasty cuff to the face that sent him sprawling. Woozily, he sat up spitting blood and croaked, "What was that fer?"

"It's to discourage ya from sneakin' off again," answered Miller. "Next time we'll hamstring ya an' be done with it!"

"How'd ya find me?" asked Jack as he eyed the sharp knife Randall waved to reinforce his brother's threat.

"We's learned a few tricks hidin' from the Injuns," snarled Rupert. "None of 'em plays fair, ya know. An' now we got one less tribe to deal with, since you an' yer pals ruined it for us with the Iroquois."

"We only kept ya from cheatin' 'em."

"An' got that old squaw's dander up."

"That was yer fault fer kickin' her. That woman ain't jess anyone. She's Dark Thunder's wife!"

"A squaw's a squaw."

"That's like sayin' a timber rattler won't bite ya. Do you know how much power Iroquois women have? They rule their families an' government an' are highly honored."

"She queered it for us with her neighborin' villages is all I know. Sent runners to every one to keep 'em from tradin' with us."

"An' now you gotta pay!" growled Randall.

"Then, why didn't ya jess give me to the Frenchies?" grumbled Jack.

"'Cause they won't torture ya like the Delaware," sneered Rupert. "Ever had a hot gun barrel shoved through yer guts?"

"No, but I've had to smell yer stink fer a week!"

"Ya won't be so brash when we trades ya at Kit-Han-Ne," assured Randall.

"So that's where we're headin'? An' here I thought you was takin' me to Fort Duquesne fer the Sunday church service."

"Ya won't crawl that far after the Lenni Lenape's done with ya," cackled Rupert, revealing his green teeth.

"Wall, let's git goin'," yelped Lightnin', "'cause at least then I'll be free o' you swine!"

"An' with the real demons! Wait 'til they ties ya to the black stake."

CHAPTER FIVE: KIT-HAN-NE

The Millers took no further chances with Jack after retrieving him from the bog. They sandwiched Hawkins between them and rudely dragged him back to the canoe. There, they bound the woodsman head-to-foot with stout rope before depositing him in the bottom of their dugout.

"Hey, what if we rolls over?" protested Lightnin' as they cast off from shore. "Tied up like this, I'll sink like a stone."

"Ya can't swim with that busted wing, anyhow, so quit yer whining!" growled Rupert, smacking Jack with his paddle.

"Shut yer trap," seconded his brother, "an' keep yer eyes peeled fer turtles. We could use a nice pot o' soup as a break from all that fish we've been eatin'."

"I know. Er you'll roast *me* fer supper instead."

The travelers continued downriver for several more days without incident. Finally, they came to a flood plain where the Allegheny widened into a more navigable expanse. Smoke rose from a village that sprawled along both banks, and Jack felt perspiration break out on his forehead when he saw it.

"Kit-Han-Ne at last!" cried Rupert. "Time to git our due."

The Millers dug feverishly for land and ploughed up on the beach next to a long string of overturned bark canoes. Once ashore, they boiled out of their craft, jerked Jack to his feet, and freed him from his bonds. Then, they straightened up his clothes and dragged a horse comb through his hair to make him more presentable.

"Ain't ya gonna fatten me up with some biscuits er somethin' before takin' me ta market?" sassed Lightnin'.

"Shut up an' come on," snarled Rupert. "Time's a wastin'."

The Millers grabbed Jack by the armpits and manhandled him up a sharp embankment. Just as they reached the crest bordering a broad cornfield below, they saw three musket-toting Indians hurrying toward them up a washed-out road. The man in the middle wore an eagle feather in his scalp lock, denoting he was a chief. He was also extremely burly, and his build reminded Hawkins of a German farmer he had met on a trading trip east of the Susquehanna. The chief's broad face wore a hostile glare, and he cocked the hammer of his gun by way of greeting.

To the sachem's left was a young boy who stared at Jack as though he were a panther ready to spring at him. The lad cocked his piece, too, and muttered a squeaky protection prayer as a further precaution.

The chief's other son stood to his right. The teen's expression was frozen in contempt of the white men, for he towered like a straight pine over them. Jack guessed the lad stood at least seven feet tall. He didn't need war paint to make him scary, for his face was sneering and his skull completely shaved.

"So traders return," grunted the sachem, totally ignoring Lightnin'. "Where are packhorses and kegs? I should take rum after how badly you cheat us last time."

"Now, hold on thar, Captain Jacobs," bleated Randall. "We come by canoe. An' without no rum."

"We got other business to chaw on," assured Rupert, nodding meaningfully toward Jack.

"No talk!" snapped Jacobs. "No business! I take sons hunting."

"But we've got a right powerful prisoner to swap ya," continued Randall. "Yer boy there sees it."

"Red Hawk only ten. Fear is his shadow. Come, Red Hawk. Young Jacobs. Family need meat, so we go."

"But what about Lightnin' Jack Hawkins? Ya don't git him handed to ya every day!" exclaimed Randall.

A glimmer of interest flared up in the chief's eyes at the mention of Jack's name. To keep the traders from noticing, he said, "Take him to village. Buffalo seen across river. We go."

Strutting like overweight roosters, the Millers prodded Hawkins down the road that skirted the broad cornfield. By the time they arrived at the cluster of log houses below, a whole mob of howling Indians had gathered to greet them.

Once the Delaware got a good look at Jack, however, a hushed silence fell over the crowd. With gasps of superstitious fear, the braves drew hatchets and knives, while their squaws and children shrank away as if from an evil presence. An old shaman began a singsong chant meant to ward off bad spirits until a diminutive chief scolded him to silence and pushed his way to the fore.

Jack recognized the new chief immediately as Shingas the Terrible by his legendary short stature. His eyes were quick as a weasel's, and his scowl was as fierce and uncompromising as his battle reputation. Shingas wore no shirt despite the chilly day, displaying arms that were sinewy and strong. From his unflinching attitude, Hawkins could see why his tribe respected him.

"Greetings, chief," said Randall, flashing a cocksure smile. "We brung ya a prisoner. An enemy you'll be happy to roast."

"An' all he'll cost ya is a stack of fine beaver plews," added Rupert. "That's for our trouble o' bringin' 'im downriver to ya."

"We not pay for return of a brother," hissed Shingas after looking Hawkins up and down.

"A brother?" echoed Randall. "Why, we found this fellow consortin' with the Iroquois at Ishua Town."

"Him show great courage the last time him with Original People. Survive gauntlet with speed and powerful medicine."

"Then, Hawkins must be a turncoat," insisted Randall, "livin' with the Iroquois, an' all."

"We solve that," answered the lean chief. "We'll adopt him."

"Adopt him?"

"Like braves of the Six Nations eat hearts of their enemies to gain their strength, we, too, become strong by making this Hawkins a Lenni Lenape."

"But we set his busted arm an' saved 'im from drownin'," protested Rupert. "You gotta give us somethin' for 'im."

"How about your lives?" grunted Shingas, yanking a scalping knife from the beaded sheath he wore around his neck. "That seem fair?"

"O-O-Oh, quite fair," stammered Randall. "T-T-Take Hawkins as a gift from us to you. W-W-

We've brought other goods to trade to your fine people. Me an' my brother will go fetch them from our canoe."

"No trade!" rumbled Shingas. "French give us all goods we need. They come soon with many bateaux of gunpowder, muskets, hatchets."

"Them sound like war supplies," croaked Randall.

"And war we give English!" yelped Shingas. "Now, be gone while I remember your gift of this Hawkins. If see you again, memory not so good. Let us wash white blood from our new brother's veins. Begin ceremony before him regain strength and use his medicine against us."

As the Millers backed carefully up the road leading from town, they watched three beautiful Indian girls slip playfully from the crowd to fetch hold of Lightnin' and strip off his trapper clothes. Hawkins' face flushed beneath his tan as they led him naked to the river and forced him to wade in up to his waist. Then, the girls, laughing with jubilant glee, scrubbed and rubbed him until his skin turned red.

A lithe, well-built lass with an extremely pretty face seemed to take special pleasure in the ceremony. She scrubbed Jack twice as hard as the other maidens while smiling deep into his eyes. Hawkins tried to fend her off, but she always kept to the side of his broken arm. Laughing flirtatiously, she dunked him under the water until he thought his lungs would burst. She continued to touch him familiarly even after her friends began leading the choking woodsman back ashore.

Watching the spectacle from their dugout canoe, Rupert griped, "Well dog my cat! We dragged that skunk Hawkins all this way expectin' revenge, an' all that happens to 'im is he gits loved to death by them squaws. Don't seem fair, it don't!"

"But there's more 'n one way to exact vengeance," growled Randall with a vicious leer spreading across his face. "I think it's time we go back upriver an' consider our options. . ."

CHAPTER SIX: SON OR PRISONER?

The Indian girls pulled the half-drowned Hawkins out of the river and ushered him up the bank. Hurrying to a longhouse at the far end of the village, they released Jack into the custody of some older squaws. After scolding the trapper to sit still, the women began plucking out his hair with little brass tweezers like he were a turkey. They continued to work until just a strip of hair remained on the top of his head. Then, the squaws threaded a new linen shirt over Jack's torso and helped him into decorated leggings and moccasins made of soft deerskin. After painting his face red and black, they seated Lightnin' on a bearskin and gave him a pipe and a hand-stitched possibles bag filled with tobacco.

Hawkins was no sooner seated when Shingas led a solemn group of elders into the council house. The Delaware were dressed in their finest clothes and were painted as though for war. They sat in a circle with Jack and began smoking until the interior of the building was filled with a blue haze. Among the tribesman Jack recognized were King Beaver, Sunfish, Cutfinger George, John Hickman, and Custaloga. He had met these Delaware at Logstown before they had gone over to the French.

Finally, the profound silence was broken when Shingas rose to address Hawkins. In a very grave voice he said, "My son, you are now flesh of our flesh, bone of our bone. By the ceremony performed this day, every drop of white blood was washed from your veins. You are now taken into the Lenni Lenape nation and adopted into a great family. My son, you have nothing to fear for we are under the same obligations to love, support, and defend you, that we are to love and defend one another."

When Shingas returned to his seat, his brother, King Beaver, stood to continue the ritual. "My son," he intoned, "we have witnessed your fleetness of foot in running our gauntlet. To honor this gift bestowed upon you by the Great Spirit, we give you the name 'Swift Lightning.' It is how you will be known in your travels with us."

After King Beaver had spoken, the elders filed out of the longhouse, and Hawkins was left to reflect upon his initiation. He was suddenly very tired and would have fallen asleep if he hadn't seen Red Hawk peeping at him from the far entrance.

Jack got to his feet in a daze and stumbled out into the noontime glare. "I thought ya went huntin' with yer pa," he said absently, while Red Hawk dodged a safe distance away.

"N-N-No. Father sent me to tell elders he want you for a s-s-son. Follow me, Swift Lightning. I I-I take you home."

A perplexed smile crossed Hawkins' face as he staggered after the youngster. No matter how hard Jack tried to catch up, Red Hawk moved a little faster to keep him two arm's lengths away. Finally, Lightnin' panted, "Stop runnin', boy. I ain't gonna hurt ya. Couldn't if I wanted to with this busted wing."

Red Hawk stopped at Jack's entreaty and grabbed him tentatively by his good arm. Then, the lad helped him stumble toward a cluster of stout log houses covered with sheets of bark.

Each dwelling made an excellent little fort, Jack noticed. There were even loopholes cut in the sides for defenders to shoot through.

Red Hawk creaked open a sturdy wooden door and escorted his new brother into the smoky one-room cabin. They padded across the dirt floor to where their mother, Willow, bent near the fireplace stirring corn soup. Jack caught a whiff of it as he entered, and his stomach churned with sudden hunger. The woman greeted Swift Lightning with a warm smile and poured him a steaming bowl of soup. "Sit," she instructed, motioning toward a wolf hide stretched in front of the glowing hearth. "Welcome, my son."

Jack ate hungrily, while the wide-eyed Red Hawk hovered next to him watching his every move. It's like this boy never saw someone chew before, thought the trapper, grinning with amusement.

After he had eaten, Hawkins thanked Willow and then said to his little brother, "How 'bout showing me 'round the village? I spent so many days ridin' in a canoe, I'd like ta stretch m' legs."

"I-I-I guess so. Is it all right, Mother?"

"Yes, go on," said Willow with a knowing shake of her head. "Only time you inside is when you sleep."

Red Hawk burst from the cabin with Swift Lightning shuffling along behind. All around them Indian boys ran races, wrestled in the dirt, or tried to outjump one another. The girls, though, chased butterflies or played with cornstalk dolls. Their laughter was music to Jack's ears, and he felt himself relax for the first time since his capture by the rum traders.

As Hawkins and his little brother meandered about Kit-Han-Ne, the trapper was quick to observe how the traditional longhouses were now replaced by clusters of log dwellings for each extended family. Captain Jacobs' people resided to the extreme left of the village, King Beaver's family was in the center, and John Hickman's dwelt to the right near a fast moving stream bordering that end of town.

"Where does Shingas live?" asked Jack when he was unable to spot the fierce chief.

"Across Allegheny," replied Red Hawk. "Him guard west door."

Hawkins also noticed a group of transient warriors had built temporary shelters between Hickman's settlement and the cornfield. These lean-tos were constructed of poles, bark, and canvas with the high side left open. Fires were built near the open entrance of each lean-to, and hostile faces huddled there to discuss an impeding raid.

Before another shelter sat a tattoo artist. He was hard at work creating small, round designs on the back of a powerful warrior's neck. Similar marks already crowded the left side of the Delaware's shaved pate.

"What are them circles for?" asked Hawkins, inching forward for a closer look.

"Heads," grunted the brave.

"Him mean 'scalps,' " added the artisan, noting the puzzled look on the woodsman's face.

Jack found the tattoo artist's work fascinating, so he squatted cross-legged to watch the skilled fellow burn tree bark into powder. The artist then pricked the warrior's skin with pike's teeth and rubbed the powder into the wound. The tattoo would be formed once the cuts healed. Jack could tell this particular brave was a steady customer, for he already had crossed lances emblazoned on his left cheek and the head of a boar on his jaw.

"Why don't you get tattoo?" asked Red Hawk, tugging excitedly on Hawkins' elbow.

"Yes," agreed the artisan. "Swift Lightning should have symbol for his prowess. Here, on right hand."

"Go ahead!" urged Jack's little brother. "It make you special."

After Hawkins nodded reluctantly, the tattoo man scored Jack's flesh with the fish teeth. It burned even worse when powder was applied, so the woodsman closed his eyes until the pain subsided. When he opened them again, he found the bold design of a winged lightning bolt stamped on his hand. Grinning with pleasure, he asked, "What's the price fer your work?"

"Bring me liver when shoot deer. Or pouch of tobacco."

Jack pulled the tobacco from his possibles bag and handed it to the artisan. Then, he and

Red Hawk headed toward the council house where his initiation had been held. As they sauntered past King Beaver's clan, Hawkins saw the same saucy girl who had half-drowned him. She was skinning a pile of muskrats, and upon spotting Jack, stopped to giggle, flirt, and bat her eyes.

Hawkins quickly looked away and muttered under his breath, "Who is that crazy squaw, Red Hawk? She makes m' flesh crawl!"

"That Little Mink," sniggered the boy. "She like you."

"Wall now, Lightnin' Jack Hawkins don't cotton to no squaws. I was born to run with the wind, an' nobody's gonna break my stride!"

"Sometimes brave had no choice in matter," teased Red Hawk, watching the girl snare his brother with her eyes.

"So here you are!" thundered a hard voice that made the little boy jump.

"Yes, Young Jacobs," whimpered Red Hawk with obvious fear. "W-W-What you want?"

Hawkins turned to find a haughty, seven-foot giant bearing down on him and his young companion. A sneer burned on the nasty fellow's lips, and he looked right through Jack before growling, "Father and me return from hunt. Find prisoner gone."

"What prisoner?"

"Him!" snarled Young Jacobs, pointing derisively toward Hawkins.

"But Swift Lightning now Lenni Lenape."

"Don't talk back," snapped the giant, drawing himself up to his full height to impress Little Mink. "Or else!"

"Come on," sniffed Red Hawk. "Better do what him say. Until I talk to Father."

As Jack followed Red Hawk back to their family home, Young Jacobs dogged their heels cursing the white hunter under his breath. Every few steps he pushed Hawkins from behind to speed him up. Lightnin' couldn't fight back because of his weakened condition. Instead, he looked furtively about to note every feature of the place that imprisoned him. In his mind a map was being drawn. In his heart escape was being longed for.

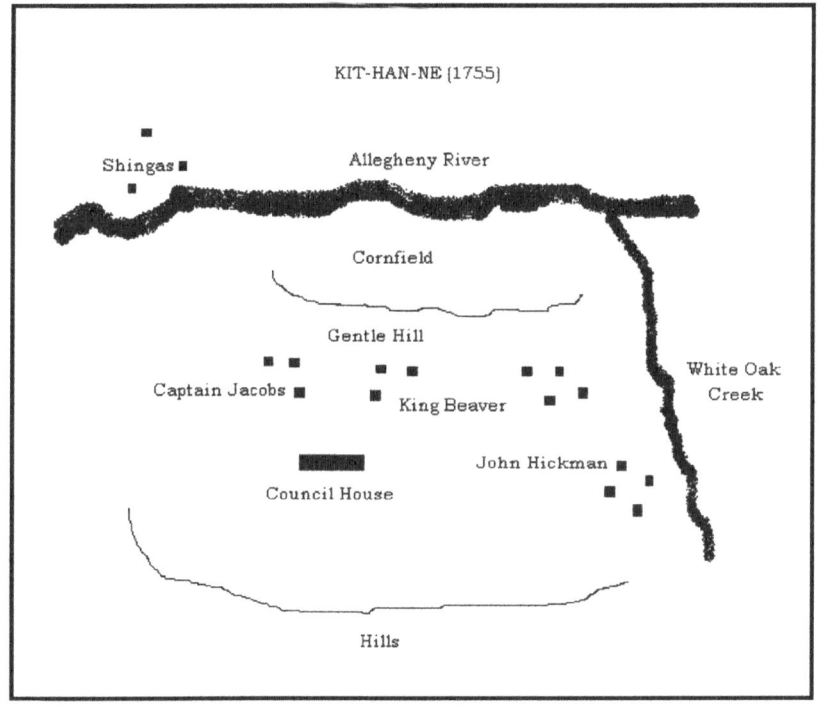

CHAPTER SEVEN:
THE FRENCH COME TO CALL

Captain Jacobs greeted Hawkins with a withering stare when he entered the family cabin accompanied by the chief's two sons. The brawny Delaware folded his strong arms over his chest and growled, "Where you been?"

"Had Red Hawk show me around, is all."

"You not to leave cabin again unless Young Jacobs go with you."

"Why's that?" asked Jack defiantly. "If you was at my adoption ceremony, you'd know I'm now a member of yer tribe. King Beaver even give me the name 'Swift Lightning.'"

"You will never be Lenni Lenape, for bond with your white friends too strong. Only captives who make good family are women and the little ones. They soon prefer our ways to those of the English."

"If ya didn't think I'd be a good son, why did ya take me in?"

"So I could watch you closer. Keep from escaping. Will never let you leave."

"Then, I am yer prisoner!" exclaimed Hawkins, glaring hard at the chief.

"Unless prefer death!" snapped Captain Jacobs, yanking a hatchet from his belt.

"Enough of this talk!" shouted Willow, scurrying between Swift Lightning and her husband to restore peace in her household. "Come. We eat. Buffalo loin now done."

Reluctantly, Captain Jacobs backed away from Hawkins. His wife offered him a wooden plate heaped with steaming meat. He snatched it from her hand and then squatted brooding by the fireplace. Young Jacobs soon joined him, while Red Hawk and Jack retreated to the far corner of the cabin to eat their supper.

The little boy stared sorrowfully at his new brother. After a moment he whispered, "Couldn't help you with Father in such rage. After him calm down, I say something."

"That's all right, Red Hawk. Don't git yerself in Dutch on my behalf. It's enough to know I got you as a friend. If you pester yer pa, he probably won't let ya talk to me at all."

The family watched the embers die on the hearth and then crawled beneath their blankets and fell asleep. Even Jack had no trouble nodding off after all the excitement of his first day in Kit-Han-Ne. His snores mingled with those of Captain Jacobs until sudden gunfire roused them on the following morning.

Boiling from his pine bough bed, the startled chief grabbed his musket and charged out the door. Jack would have followed him if Young Jacobs hadn't swung his long foot under his and sent him sprawling. Before Hawkins could spring up again, Captain returned with a wide grin wreathed on his face. "French here," he said. "Bring many gifts for Delaware."

The sachem, accompanied by Young Jacobs, struck out for the council house across the way. There, a French officer in a white uniform coat was directing a company of militien who were carting kegs of black powder into the village. These militia were dressed in leather leggings, bleached linen smocks, and pointy knit caps. The grunts and foreign curses that accompanied their labor caused Jack and Red Hawk to peer curiously out the door of the Jacobs' house at them.

The French had no sooner set down their burdens in the yard outside the longhouse when Shingas and a mob of howling warriors rushed from the far side of the village to greet their allies. "Now, we have enough powder to wage ten year war with English!" yelped the chief. "Let us hide our store throughout Kit-Han-Ne, so all braves have good supply."

To carry out Shingas' order, the kegs were divided among the families of the Wolf clan and carefully stowed away in the homes of their chiefs. Two barrels were stashed in Captain Jacobs' cabin, and Jack breathed a sign of relief when he saw that the powder was kept well away from the fireplace.

In the meantime, the French militia brought boxes of rifles, flints, hatchets, and other supplies into Kit-Han-Ne. After each brave had taken what he needed, Shingas led his men in a wild war dance. Armed with tomahawks and knives, they contorted their faces like fiends and threatened to strike each other. Around and around they whirled portraying a frantic battle, while Shingas sang of his past deeds and those of his ancestors. When the dance had reached a fever pitch, the warriors struck a post with their weapons. Delirium flashed in their eyes, and wolf howls rattled in their throats. The pandemonium caused Hawkins' face to go pale as he relived his run through the gauntlet and his brush with death.

After the war dance, a wild celebration swept through Kit-Han-Ne when a feast was prepared in honor of the French allies. Tables were assembled along the walls of the council house, and beaming squaws piled them with huge quantities of food. Soon, everyone gorged on venison, bear meat, and a thick stew while sharing laughter and good fellowship. The guests made the evening livelier when they broke out a keg of rum and passed it out freely to the Delaware.

Devoting all his efforts to guzzling liquor, Young Jacobs even forgot to bully Hawkins. That allowed Jack to watch enthralled as the tribe formed into concentric circles in the center of the council house to begin a social dance. The innermost circle was made up of men, the second of women, and the third of more braves. To the throbbing beat of a hollow log drum, the men leaped, jumped, wailed, and stomped their feet until the ground shook. The women, though, moved gracefully while tapping their feet to the rhythm. They slid one foot forward and then backward, keeping their bodies straight. Their arms hung at their sides, and, in direct contrast to the wailing warriors, they did not speak.

The women's silence did not prevent Little Mink from sending a clear message to Hawkins. She danced directly in front of his table gazing longingly into his face until he returned her stare. She was dressed in her finest deerskin shirt decorated with red and yellow ribbons. Her dark hair glistened in the firelight, which accented the glistening necklace she had made from bits of wampum, silver, and deer antlers. But her real beauty shone from her face, and she flashed Jack a bright smile filled with straight, white teeth.

The dance continued for what seemed to Hawkins like hours, while Little Mink made eyes at him. He squirmed uncomfortably and wished someone would offer him a cup of rum. She wiggled ever closer until he detected the tinkling of the bells she wore around her ankles. The sound became oppressive as her shadow crept to engulf him.

As soon as the drum grew silent, Lightnin' looked wild-eyed for an exit. Little Mink was now only a few feet away, and he caught a whiff of her musky odor. It was then that Young Jacobs leaped from his seat to snatch hold of the maiden's hand. Drunkenly, he embraced her until she pushed him away in disgust. After sharply rebuking the chief's son, she pointed to Jack and said, "I'm his. You stay away!"

A jealous fire flared up in Young Jacobs' eyes, and he staggered around the table to manhandle Hawkins out the longhouse door. With each step the giant took, he kicked Jack on the back of his legs to hurry him along.

Finally, the woodsman whirled to face his antagonist. "To think I'm hers, that squaw must be drunker 'n you," he snapped. "Or maybe she's addled in the brain. I don't like her. No way, no how!"

"You lie!" roared Young Jacobs. "Little Mink most beautiful girl on Allegheny. How can you not love her?"

Young Jacobs took a wild swing at Swift Lightning's head. Jack dodged at the last instant, and the soused teen spun heavily to the ground. Before the drunk could regain his feet, Hawkins raced to the Jacobs' house where he found Willow making corn bread for the French.

"Sit down, my son," she said kindly. "You pant like winded, old horse. You must rest yourself if want arm to heal. Take off sling and let me see."

Hawkins did as he was instructed, and his Indian mother gently massaged his aching injury. Then, she prepared a soothing plaster made of wintergreen and mustard to bring heat to the area. When Young Jacobs came bursting into the cabin to renew his confrontation with Jack, he was hushed to silence by Willow and sent to bed.

CHAPTER EIGHT: BLACK FISH

The next morning the French militia and a hundred very groggy braves assembled in the middle of town. The Delaware were painted for war, and their faces glistened with hideous streaks of red and black. All were heavily armed with muskets, knives, hatchets, and war clubs, too, and Hawkins shuddered as he watched them from the doorway of the Jacobs' house.

Shingas and Captain Jacobs conferred briefly with the French officer, Chevalier Villiers, over a crudely-drawn map in the dirt. After discussing their strategy, the chiefs divided the men into two war parties. Then, Shingas raised his arms to the sky to address the Great Spirit in a humble prayer:

O poor me!
Who am going out to fight the enemy
And know not whether I shall return again
To enjoy the embraces of my children
And my wife.

O thou Great Spirit above!
Take pity on my children and on my wife!
Prevent their mourning on my account!
Grant that I may be successful in this attempt.

O take pity on me!
Give me strength and courage to meet my enemy.
Suffer me to return again to my children,
And I will make thee a sacrifice.

Solemnly, Shingas joined his war party and led it to the Allegheny to board awaiting canoes. Captain Jacobs and the Frenchman Villiers, meanwhile, marched their force down a much-traveled trail to the east. That left Young Jacobs and a handful of teenage boys in charge of Kit-Han-Ne.

Instead of posting sentries around the perimeter of town, the youths returned to the council house to finish the rum left from the night before. Their laughter became louder with each cup they drank, and to pass the time, they began a spirited game of black fish. Jack had been tied up before play began, and he craned his neck to see if he could learn the rules. He was about to give up when Red Hawk slipped to his side and moved him into a better position to observe the action.

From his new vantage point, Hawkins immediately learned that black fish was a gambling game played by a circle of contestants. Each contestant had a pile of beads sitting next to him that he used for chips. At the beginning of each round, players placed one chip in the pot.

Long Arrow, the first player, was a lean, agile youth with intense eyes. He held a turtle shell filled with game pieces in his quick hands. The pieces included four flat round rocks and two fish-shaped shale stones. Each was painted black on one side and left plain on the other.

Long Arrow gripped the turtle shell by the rim and shook it madly until the stones flew upward into the air. With the reflexes of a cat, he jerked the shell back under the game pieces before they could hit the ground. One fish skidded up the rim and would have squirted out if the nimble lad hadn't tilted the turtle shell at the last instant.

Red Hawk exhaled sharply and then applauded Long Arrow's dexterity. Whispering to Jack, he said, "That was close call! If even one stone fall to ground, him receive no points and lose turn."

"Well, how do ya score in this here game?" asked Hawkins.

"Each flat stone land plain side up, count one point. Black side, no points. Fish landing plain side up equal two points. If all six pieces black or plain, get ten points. But look! Long Arrow have two black fish in shell. Him must give up turn with no points."

"What if a fellow had two white fish?"

"Then, get six points for fish plus score from plain rocks. Also <u>must</u> toss again. That get more score for player, or he lose all if don't catch rocks or have two black fish."

Dejectedly, Long Arrow passed the turtle shell to Young Jacobs, the player on his left. The giant, however, had been drinking much more than his friends and could barely shake the shell. After finally managing to launch the game pieces skyward, he clumsily caught them with a last gasp, spastic movement. Somehow, all the pieces landed safely, black side up.

When Young Jacobs saw that he had scored ten points, he flashed a greedy grin. After shoving the shell under the other contestants' noses, he shook it a second time. Dumb luck was on his side again because all the pieces landed white side up, giving him another ten points. Boasting "Me great; me win," he attempted a third turn, only to have a fish ricochet off his wrist and fall in slow motion to the dirt beside him.

Young Jacobs bellowed in rage and pitched the game pieces to the next player. After pounding the ground in drunken frustration, he downed yet another full cup of rum.

Snickering at the bully's misfortune, Jack asked Red Hawk, "What happens now?"

"Play continue until someone score most points. Him get beads in pot. Then, start new round. They play and play until one has all beads. Him win what others bet at beginning of black fish game."

What Young Jacobs bet and lost was the new musket he was given by the French soldiers. When he handed it to the jubilant Two Crows, the giant yelped, "You cheat! You not drink like rest of us. That give you advantage. You gulp rum before next game."

"But can't play new game," lamented Long Arrow. "Lost furs I trapped. Have nothing to bet."

"Lost all my gunpowder," cried Rushing Bear. "Can't play, either."

"Then, we play for him!" sneered the giant, pointing toward Jack Hawkins.

"Him?" inquired Rushing Bear.

"Winner get him. To torture!"

A whoop rattled from the throats of the other inebriated youths, and they began to dance madly around Hawkins, waving their knives inches from his face and torso. While Jack sat unflinching through their dervish, Red Hawk burst out the door of the longhouse and sped home.

Winded from their drunken exercise, the Indians collapsed into a circle to play one round for Jack's hide. Long Arrow again gripped the turtle shell in his hands and carefully swirled the game pieces before flinging them skyward. This time, one of the fish landed white side up, giving him two points. He also got four more points for the plain stones he secured in the shell.

Smiling broadly, Long Arrow passed the game to Young Jacobs. With sweat glistening on his saturnine face, the giant concentrated mightily before casting the game pieces. Driven by hate, he easily captured them in the shell. His lips twisted in a sadistic leer when he rose to show Hawkins the six black stones that had turned things in his favor. Drawing his knife, he pretended to slit his nostrils and cut off his forefinger. Then, he handed the turtle shell to Two Crows and grunted, "Beat ten!"

Two Crows had been forced by the others to swill three cups of rum before his turn. Not good at holding his liquor, he spilled the stones before he could hurl them into the air. The next three players weren't much better, so Rushing Bear became Jack's only hope for besting his vicious brother.

Rushing Bear took the turtle shell, swirled the stones, and flung them with surety. He caught them with equal confidence and found one white fish, one black fish, and four black discs in the shell. That gave him only two points but the chance to continue his turn. Twice more he tried his luck but still found himself one point shy of Young Jacobs' total.

Gulping with dismay, Rushing Bear flung the stones skyward a fourth time. The two fish returning to the shell smacked together sending them dangerously to the edge of the rim. Just as they were about to squirt to the ground, the youth saved them with a lunge and a swirl. Peering expectantly into the bottom of the shell, he found two black fish staring up at him. With a deflated groan, he hurled the game against the wall, scattering the pieces everywhere.

Leaping victoriously to his feet, Young Jacobs again produced his scalping knife. He waved it slowly in front of Jack's eyes and then slashed it viciously the full length of Hawkins' cheek. "See how pretty Little Mink find you now!" shrieked the bully. "See--"

Before Young Jacobs could continue the torture, Willow rushed into the council house to smack him with her broom. After knocking the knife from her reeling son's hand, she walloped him alongside the head and drove him out the door with repeated blows to his backside.

Afterward, she turned her rage on the drunken youngsters who sat gaping at her with open mouths. "Get up!" Willow ranted. "Go on watch! Village unsafe without you guarding it. Go!"

While the young bucks filed crestfallen from the longhouse to obey their clan mother, Willow stooped to free Hawkins from his bonds. "That nasty gash on your face," she said with a concerned frown. "Come, now. I tend your cut. Take care of Young Jacobs, too!"

(Photo courtesy of Randy Quinn)

CHAPTER NINE: MORE GAMES

After Willow put Young Jacobs in his place, Jack led a more peaceful existence among the Delaware. He was allowed to go out again with just Red Hawk accompanying him, and they spent many fun hours fishing in the Allegheny using hand lines and birds' claws for hooks. They also swam often together, splashing and laughing in the chilly water. The only one who disquieted Swift Lightning now was the omnipresent Little Mink. It seemed that every time he dove naked into the river, she was there to ogle him.

When snow signaled the approach of an early winter, Hawkins spent his evenings in the sweat lodge to get more healing heat on his arm. Dressed only in a loin cloth, he entered the small framed structure that was covered with several layers of tree bark to insulate it. Using tongs, he carefully placed hot stones in a central pit and poured water on them to create steam. The woodsman could feel his bones knit with each steam bath he took. He was good as new by the middle of November.

One morning Jack said to his little brother, "With the hard winter comin' fast, I want to teach ya a white man's game. Then, we'll have somethin' to do when we's shut in all the time."

"What game is that?"

"It's called 'checkers.' "

"It not like black fish, is it?" squeaked Red Hawk, recoiling with fear.

"No! No!" laughed Hawkins. "It's real relaxin'. Nobody bets nothin', an' nobody gits mad when he loses. To make the game, though, I need ya to fetch me some things from the woods where I ain't allowed to go."

"What things?"

"Some birch an' cherry bark to make our game pieces an' pine pitch to glue 'em together. I'll also need sharp stones to cut with."

"Why don't I get you knife?"

"No, yer pa wouldn't want me to have no weapon. He'd punish us fer sure! Now, git goin' while I make us a checker board."

As soon as Red Hawk lit out for the woods, Jack sifted through a pile of furs in the corner of the cabin until he found a brain tanned deer hide that was smooth and soft. Stretching it out on the floor in front of the fireplace, he used charred sticks to draw sixty-four small squares on the hide. Half of the squares he colored black. The other half he left plain. He had just finished his labor when his little brother burst in the door with the other things he needed.

"Boy, that was quick!" exclaimed Hawkins. "It's you who should be called 'Lightning.'"

"Got stones and pitch from arrow maker," panted Red Hawk, "and bark from edge of woods. Can I help make pieces?"

"Sure!"

Jack cut the red and white bark into circles of equal size and had his brother glue like-colored disks together two-high to make them thicker. After they had fashioned twelve red pieces and twelve white pieces, Hawkins said, "Now, we're ready to play."

"Hey, I want red!" yelped the boy. "It in my name."

"Then, ya must have played this here game before," teased Jack, "'cause the dark color always goes first."

"No! No! What do I do?"

"Place all yer pieces on the dark squares o' the board startin' at the top. I'll do the same at the bottom with my white ones."

"All right!"

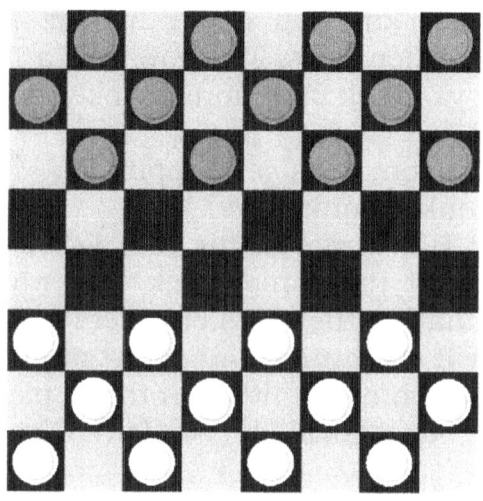

"Now, think o' the board as a pond full o' lily pads an' yer pieces as frogs."

"Frogs?"

"Yes, 'cause to capture the other player's checkers, ya gotta jump over 'em."

"Are they greenies or bullfrogs?" giggled Jack's little brother.

"Both," chuckled Hawkins. "I'll explain later. First, though, you gotta hop one o' yer frogs forward to another black lily pad. The white pads ain't strong enough ta hold yer frog's weight, so ya can't land there. Ya kin only move one frog one pad at a time. If he ends up next to one o' my white frogs an' the pad behind it is open, you jump over my fellow an' gaff him from the pond."

"This does sound like fun!"

"An' it gits way more interestin' when yer greenies grow up inta bullfrogs."

"How does that happen?"

"One o' yer boys has to work his way to the bottom row of lily pads where my last row o' white frogs is now. Then, he grows inta a full-sized gronker that kin hop backward an' forward ta stomp out other frogs. To show he's a full-growed king frog, ya stack one more checker on top of yer champeen."

"Come on. Let's get hopping!"

"Gronk! Gronk!"

Red Hawk moved his red pieces very recklessly to start the game. Jack took no mercy on him, eliminating the boy's checkers right and left. When Swift Lightning made a multiple jump, wiping out two of his little brother's pieces in one turn, the boy squealed, "No fair! Give back red frogs."

"I play by the rules," insisted Jack. "I kin keep hoppin' as long as there's a black lily pad behind each o' yer greenies."

"Then, take this!" shouted Red Hawk triumphantly, jumping his red checker over three of Jack's. "And look where I land. I now bullfrog! Stack me one higher. And watch out!"

"Gronk! Gronk!"

The brothers lounged in front of the fireplace all afternoon playing checkers. The games went back and forth so many times that all that mattered in the end was the laughter and frog noises they shared. They made so much commotion that finally Young Jacobs tromped into the cabin to investigate. When he saw the board game stretched between them, he reached down and swept it with one motion into the fire.

"What'd ya do that fer?" growled Hawkins, leaping angrily to his feet.

"Yes!" howled Red Hawk, bursting into tears. "We only having fun."

"It look to me like you gamble," grunted the giant, glowering down at his brothers.

"Gamble?" repeated Jack, clenching his fists.

"Mother forbid black fish. Say bad!"

"But this was checkers," sputtered Hawkins.

"No matter. All gambling bad!"

"Oh, what the hell. Come on, Red Hawk. Let's go fishin'."

After Jack and his little brother had snatched up their hand lines and stormed outside, Red Hawk sniffed, "Why you let Young Jacobs burn our game? Your arm strong, now. Should have hit him."

"I woulda done just that," replied Swift Lightning softly, "only yer ma don't approve o' fightin' in her house. It was mighty hard holdin' my temper. I reckon I only done it out o' respect fer Willow."

"Way Young Jacobs treat you, you should run off. Be with your people."

"Not when I'm out with you," said Jack, putting his arm around Red Hawk's shoulder. "Then, you'd get blamed fer not watchin' me proper."

CHAPTER TEN: THE RAIDERS RETURN

When Jack and Red Hawk returned to the Jacobs' home, Hawkins said, "I need to rest fer a while. Why don't ya see if there's any salt left from the supply the Frenchies brung us? Then, ya might go snare a rabbit to put it on."

"I'm hungry, too," replied the boy. "Didn't catch fish. Have better luck in woods."

Jack stepped inside the log house and, to his relief, found Willow and Young Jacobs gone. Just as he hoped, the leftover supplies he had used to make checkers were also where he had hid them. Examining the stones his brother had gotten from the arrow maker, he chose the sharpest one and used it to split a spare broom handle his Indian mother kept near the fireplace. Next, he inserted the stone point into the handle to fashion a spear. He secured the spear head with twine and pine pitch. When he had finished, he tested the spear's balance before whispering, "This here's a weapon Will Cutler would be proud of."

Jack then crept to his corner of the family cabin and changed into his winter moccasins. Made with the fur on the inside, they would keep his feet nice and warm on his trek to Ishua Town. After pulling on his buckskin shirt and beaver robe, he slipped out the door and slunk toward the wooded hill he could just see beyond the council house. He wanted to be gone before Red Hawk came back, so his little brother couldn't be punished for allowing him to escape.

Hawkins had just reached the shadows of the longhouse wall when the shrill cries of "Aw Ohhhhhh! Ah Ohhhhhhhh! Ah Ohhhhhhhhhh!" announced the return of Shingas the Terrible's warriors from their winter raid. Over and over the braves repeated their hair-raising calls until they accounted for each head taken. To Jack, these halloos blended the elements of triumph and fear, and he watched mesmerized as the war party emerged from the forest waving the scalps of their victims on the end of thin poles.

The warriors led a string of ragged, cringing prisoners into the village. Most were scared women and children whose hands were bound with stout rope. Hawkins recognized the Martin family whom he had met at Great Cove while on a hunting trip there. Mrs. Martin wore a frozen, dazed expression on her face like she was sleepwalking through hell. The middle girl, Martha, carried her bawling two year old sister, while her small brothers slogged along staring at their snowy shoes. Only pretty Mary was at all animated as she fended off the repeated advances of a tall warrior at her side.

When the prisoners, thirteen in all, had been herded into the center of town, the warriors formed two lines and began goading the older male captives to run between them. Each brave waved a war club, hatchet, or rifle stock, and Jack's brain sent him a steady stream of flashbacks from his own race through the dreaded gauntlet. These men, however, displayed no grit at all. When the first husband firmly refused Shingas' command to run, the angry chief ran his scalping knife across the coward's throat. As the fellow fell dead to the ground, his bright blood sprayed across the face of his shrieking wife.

The second white man wasn't so lucky. He no sooner fainted into the snow when King Beaver and John Hickman skidded him like a log to the black torture pole. After ripping the scalp from the whimpering fool's head, they jerked him upright and tied him to the stake. It was then that Long Arrow, Rushing Bear, and the sneering Young Jacobs came bolting from a nearby house to start a roaring fire. Setting splinters of wood ablaze, they stuck them in the white husband's arms and cackled with delight at his wails of anguish. King Beaver then carved off the man's ears and fingers and forced them into his mouth until he swallowed them. Blood pulsed from the finger stubs, increasing the victim's agony.

When it seemed to Jack that the torture had reached its climax, John Hickman sliced a hole in the craven husband's stomach and pulled out part of his intestines. After cutting the man loose from the torture stake, King Beaver dragged him to a skinny maple. There, he tied his victim's guts around the trunk and drove him around and around in circles until he unraveled all his insides. Being he still did not die, several braves heated their musket barrels and shoved them through his quivering body.

The husband screamed until his voice gave out. Finally, in a hoarse whisper he croaked, "Water, please, a drink of water."

Instead, Young Jacobs melted some lead in a pot and poured it down the captive's throat. The stench was as horrible as the man's last gurgles, and Hawkins felt his queasiness turn to outrage. It took all of his willpower to stay hidden in the shadows as he clutched his spear in a death grip.

(Photo courtesy of Greg Rearick)

Jack barely had time to absorb the brutality of the white husband's death when Many Shots, the young Delaware who had dragged Mary

Martin into camp, suddenly stepped forward with his hostage. He was an extremely handsome brave with a well-chiseled physique, and the young Indian women in the crowd gazed at him with adoring eyes. The girl, too, was of uncommon beauty, and the maidens hissed in rage when Many Shots said, "Chief Shingas, it my wish to marry this women I take from Great Cove. Look how strong her bones. How wide her hips. She give me fine sons to hunt meat and provide for Lenni Lenape."

Many Shots' speech concluded in howls of indignant jealousy, and young squaws poured from every corner of camp to drag the Martin girl away from him and fall upon her with flailing fists and branches they wrenched from trees. The brave stood gaping as his prospective bride was pummeled into a bloody pulp. Shingas didn't interfere in this beating. Young Jacobs crowded closer so as not to miss a single punch.

Little Mink's absence was the only surprise to Jack Hawkins as he watched with loathing the death of Mary Martin. Having seen enough of the Delaware's cruel ways, he turned and bolted for the wooded hills as though his feet were on fire. He had only gotten half-way to the safety of the forest when he recognized Long Arrow's shrill voice trailing after him. Soon, the whole village erupted with war cries as Shingas' braves came streaming past the council house after him. Jack immediately threw off his robe, so he could run faster.

With fresh visions of roasting flesh and dangling entrails pushing him on, Lightnin' weaved through the oaks in blind fear. He could hear his pursuers gaining with every passing moment until Little Mink appeared suddenly at his side and took his hand. Crashing off to the right, she led him to a smooth trail where his fleetness could serve him better. It only took Jack three steps to hit full stride, and he pulled away from the maiden in ten. He could hear her sprinting along behind him with her breath rasping in her throat as he tore along full-bore for another mile.

Finally, Jack came out on the bank of the broad Allegheny. To his surprise, Little Mink had somehow caught up to him and was now only a couple strides behind. There were more running feet besides, and Hawkins glanced hard over his shoulder to see Young Jacobs, Rushing Bear, Long Arrow, and two other teenage boys hard on their heels. All were armed with hatchets, and hate glistened on their sweaty faces.

Jack halted abruptly and let Little Mink pass him. Then, he flung his spear with all his might toward his weasel of a brother. The missile stuck in the ground directly between Young Jacobs' feet, and he tripped headlong in front of the other speeding youths. With no time to stop or veer, Long Arrow and Rushing Bear fell heavily over their gangly leader, knocking the wind from their lungs. In another instant, the trail was littered with twisted bodies, and Lightnin' whirled to follow the girl's musky scent.

Hawkins and his companion ran until the shadows of evening engulfed them. Twice, they were forced to dive into the brush when canoes full of searching braves glided down the river beside them. Another time their progress was impeded when Jack carried Little Mink across an icy stream that burst down a mountain to flood the path. Nearing exhaustion, he smiled at the memory of his brother's clumsy tumble that had bought them a little breathing room.

(Photo courtesy of Gary T. Gibson)

Just as the moonless night ended all travel, the runners concealed themselves beneath the trunk of a windfall. Shivering with cold, they puffed and wheezed until their breath returned to normal. Finally, Hawkins whispered through chattering teeth, "Thank ya, Little Mink, fer, you know. . .savin' my hide. Why in thunder did ya do it, anyhow?"

"Great Spirit visit me in dream," murmured the girl, snuggling closer to Jack. "Him tell me you coming. That you be mine."

"B-B-But now you'll never be able ta return to yer people. Why, they'd cut ya in pieces an' feed ya to the dogs!"

"You my people," answered the girl, closing her soft hand around his wrist.

"No, I'm Lightnin' Jack Hawkins, an' I don't want a squaw slowin' me down. I was born to be free as an eagle flyin' over the hills."

"You still free. But now, there are two eagles. Flying side-by-side."

CHAPTER ELEVEN: HIDE AND SEEK

Lightnin' woke at first light to find himself covered with a dusting of white flakes. Shaking Little Mink awake, he muttered, "Now, we's in a real fix, girl. Look at all the fresh trackin' snow that come down. An' we can't escape by the river, neither, with all them canoes sniffin' fer us."

"Come," replied the maiden, flashing Jack an encouraging smile. "I know place where tracks no show. We be safe. You see."

Little Mink crawled stiffly from beneath the deadfall, stretched her lithe body, and then led Hawkins down a side trail away from the Allegheny. They entered a dense pine forest that the flurries couldn't penetrate and, sure enough, discovered bare ground. Here, they slipped silently along being careful not to leave footprints or muss the pine needles. The going was slow but steady, and the whisper of their moccasins did nothing to disturb the chirping birds.

The travelers continued along until midday when Hawkins motioned toward a thicket. There, they concealed themselves to munch on corn bread the girl had brought in her deerskin pouch.

"Looks like we fool 'em," whispered Little Mink gleefully, entwining her arm around Jack's.

"Ain't so sure," mumbled Lightnin'. "You best keep yer eyes peeled an' pray to that Great Spirit you's so familiar with."

After Hawkins' warning, the young couple sat eating in silence to watch a flock of nuthatches flutter through the bushes. The birds cackled happily as they hung upside down and feasted on beechnuts. Suddenly, the flock scattered, and Jack strained his ears until he heard a rustle of movement. Peering carefully from the brush, he spied a party of Delaware creeping along the trail hunting for their sign. These weren't boys but seasoned warriors armed with muskets and woods savvy. Often, they stopped to examine scuffs in the dirt and confer among themselves.

When the search party drew even with the fugitives' hiding place, Jack felt Little Mink's hand tighten around his. Lightnin' shook her off and crouched low, coiling his legs beneath him. His lips curled into a snarl as he readied himself to spring at the first brave that should discover them.

The Delaware again held a brief conference conducted with pointed fingers and hand signals. After the longest time, they slipped off down the path, sniffing the air like hounds. It wasn't until they disappeared around a turn in the trail that Hawkins allowed himself to breathe again.

Jack and Little Mink waited another ten minutes before they emerged from hiding. Then, they turned and ran for all they were worth back toward the river. It had grown much colder now, and the sprinters exhaled plumes of icy breath as they raced along. They had almost reached the border of the forest when some deep instinct warned Hawkins to put on the brakes.

Jack skidded to a halt, leaving a long gouge in the ground. Snatching up a pine branch, he brushed away his moccasin smudge and then doubled over to catch his breath. Little Mink looked exhausted, too. Drool spilt from the corner of her gasping mouth, and her eyes had an empty cast to them.

"We best be movin'," whispered Hawkins over his thundering heartbeat. "No tellin' when them warriors will backtrack after us."

"Then, I fight," hissed Little Mink, yanking a flint knife from her pouch. "No one take you from me."

Jack and the girl again assumed a careful gait. It had gotten bitter cold, and frozen twigs snapped with every footstep. Sticking to the shadows, they flitted along until they reached the main trail that followed the Allegheny. Here, they left distinct footprints going both directions on the snowy path. They also walked in circles to create a veritable maze of tracks that struck off in every direction of the compass. When they had finished this deception, they crept into a patch of laurel to hide themselves.

The couple had just slid on their bellies when the tramping of a large number of feet reached their ears. Soon, they saw Captain Jacobs puffing like an out-of-breath bear. He was stomping along at the head of a weary contingent of Delaware braves and French militia. There was also a ragged herd of white captives, many of whom sported lash marks from where they'd been whipped along like cattle. Several testy warriors still cracked lengths of rope at the boys lagging at the rear of the column.

Before the chief's war party reached the intersection of the two trails, Young Jacobs came hobbling toward it from the direction of Kit-Han-Ne. He was accompanied by a frantic Rushing Bear who motioned toward Hawkins' and Little Mink's tracks in the snow. "Stop! Stop!" he yelled. "No come farther, or stamp out Swift Lightning's sign!"

"Swift Lightning?" growled Captain Jacobs. "What he do out here?"

"Him escape," confessed the chief's son. "With Little Mink. Almost caught them, but. . .he trip me."

"Trip you?" frothed Jacobs, reaching up to smack his namesake across the face. "What are you--woman?"

"No-o-o, Father!"

"Then, find him and his squaw!"

A look of shame and anger crossed Young Jacobs' face before he and Rushing Bear peeled off into the brush. Then, the chief signaled to his best scouts, and they sniffed around the tracked up snow for several minutes before a disagreement broke out as to where they should pursue the runaways. Spewing curses, Captain Jacobs finally sent warriors scrambling in every direction to comb the woods.

That left the chief with only two braves to help him drive the captives to Kit-Han-Ne. Taking advantage of this lack of guards, three stone-faced brothers backed nearly to a bend in the trail before being corralled by the furious sachem. Then, a distraught lass fled for the woods only to be overtaken by a fleeter savage. Order wasn't restored until Captain Jacobs threatened to split the squalling girl's skull with his hatchet. Then, he howled, "I kill all who run and all who stay if happen again!"

Hawkins watched tensely as the Delaware goaded their quaking prisoners away through the forest. He didn't rise from the brush, however, until squirrels appeared in the nearby pines to celebrate Captain Jacobs' departure. Cheered by their happy chatter, Jack helped Little Mink to her feet, and they slipped toward the Allegheny. It had grown so cold that ice floes dotted the dark water by the time they reached the river.

"No canoes now," snickered Jack, suppressing his shivers. "That ice would knock a hole through elm bark."

"But how we get away?" croaked the girl, glancing furtively into the gloomy copse behind them.

"How 'bout buildin' a raft? Look at all the driftwood on the bank there. Ice can't sink that."

"I get vines to lash trees together," murmured Little Mink, pulling out her flint knife. "You hurry."

To ease the girl's anxiety, Hawkins scrambled down the icy shore and began untangling logs that had been twisted into a pile there by the fury of the spring river. He dragged the dead timber to a beach behind him, only choosing the lightest pieces that were easier to haul and sure to float. When he had gathered enough wood for the raft, he found two ten foot saplings that he bent to the ground and cut with a sharp rock. They would use these poles for pushing and steering.

Once everything was ready, Jack stood with a pole in his hand staring expectantly into the dark evening forest. He didn't wait long before the brush parted and out strode Young Jacobs and Rushing Bear shoving Little Mink before them at gunpoint. When they emerged onto the beach, the giant wrapped his arm around the girl's throat to keep her from bolting to Hawkins. Rushing Bear, meanwhile, aimed his musket at the woodsman's heart and grunted, "Now, we got you, Swift Lightning. See how fast you escape this time!"

The taunt had no sooner left the smug brave's lips when Jack lashed out with his long staff to slap the gun away from his foe. To retaliate, Young Jacobs cocked his piece with his free hand. Before he could discharge it, Little Mink bit him so viciously on the left forearm that he yipped in surprise and dropped the musket.

Lightnin' then sprung at Young Jacobs with the quickness of an enraged panther. Flinging the girl aside, the bully drew his hatchet and swung wildly past the flying trapper's ear. Jack hit him in the chest with all his might, and the two combatants rolled over and over spraying snow in all directions. Rushing Bear retrieved his weapon but found it useless with the barrel plugged with slush. Before he could draw his knife and dive to his friend's aid, Little Mink felled him with a hard kick to the kneecap.

In desperation Young Jacobs gouged at Jack's eyes and bit him on the ear. The squirting blood only made Hawkins more determined.

Wrenching the hatchet from his enemy's hand, he bludgeoned him heavily with the blunt end until he quit squirming.

"You best git them vines, Little Mink," huffed Jack as he rose to knock out Rushing Bear with a kick to the face.

"I-I-Is Young Jacobs. . .dead?" quavered the girl, favoring her bruised throat.

"I reckon not. I didn't cut him none, even though he de-served it. Now, he'll have to answer to his pa fer failin' ag'in. That's punishment enough. Go!"

Little Mink jerked the scalping knife from the unconscious Rushing Bear's sheath and scurried away to do Jack's biding. She returned moments later with a roll of flexible vines that she and Hawkins used to tie together the logs of their crude raft. Afterward, they skidded it onto the shore ice jutting into the river. Jack set the poles on board and then helped Little Mink climb onto the deck. It was easy pushing across the ice, and well before darkness fell, Hawkins successfully launched them into the black current.

CHAPTER TWELVE: A COLD RIVER RIDE

It didn't take long for Jack and Little Mink to discover that their raft was at the mercy of the swift-flowing river. No matter how desperately they pushed with their poles, the current sucked them in a different direction. The channel was filling with slush ice, too, and steel blue cakes of it banged against the logs beneath their feet. The concussions threatened to smash their craft and cast them at any second into the frigid Allegheny.

Just as dusk fell upon them, Jack spied an island looming from the murk ahead. Gesturing madly toward it, he shouted, "Steer there, Little

Mink! Fort Duquesne ain't far downstream. If we float by them French cannon, we'll be in a real pickle!"

The raftsman and the girl pushed with their poles until the veins stood out in their necks. After many minutes of intense effort, they swung their craft into direct line with the rocky isle. Before they reached its shore, however, a huge block of ice bore down on them from the rear. Spying this danger at the last instant, Jack wheeled to fend it off. He jammed his pole hard into the ice, and it wedged in a crevice. Before he yanked his staff free, the floe shot past, dragging Hawkins into the water with a dull splash.

Lightnin' felt the air rush from his lungs as the frigid river enveloped him. Instantly, his legs went numb, and he grasped for the raft with panic glittering in his eyes. Somehow, his hand closed over a log, and he clung to it madly until Little Mink gripped him by the wrist and wrest him aboard.

Jack's buckskins were sheeted with ice by the time he hit the deck. His lips were blue, and his eyes rolled back in his head. The girl collapsed on top of him and rubbed his arms and legs to restore the circulation. "Lightning! Lightning!" she yelped. "I not let you freeze!"

Little Mink's cries were interrupted by a terrible crunch as the raft slammed hard into the island bank. The jolt sent its occupants sailing onto the shore where they hit with a thud on the sloping rocks. The raft itself was knocked into matchsticks and swept away downstream.

The couple no sooner landed when they started sliding backward into the icy current. The girl was still on top of Jack, and she latched hold of a boulder just as her toes touched the drink.

Fueled by adrenaline, she clung to the rock until she had stopped Hawkins' slide. Then, she clawed her way uphill dragging his dead weight behind her.

Once safely ashore, Little Mink tore off Jack's frozen clothes and wrapped her cloak around him. Feverishly, she dug flint and steel from her pouch to strike sparks into a pile of twigs she snapped from a dead tree. When a small blaze sprung to life, she added driftwood until flames leaped high into the dark sky.

The girl dragged her man close to the fire and resumed rubbing his extremities to keep the blood flowing. When Jack's eyes regained their luster, she forced him to his feet and helped him stagger around and around the licking flames. By daybreak Hawkins felt much better, and he hugged Little Mink to show her his appreciation.

Jack dried his buckskins over the fire until they quit smoking. As he pulled them on, he glanced across the river to the far shore. Then, he gave his girlfriend another hug and blabbed, "Well, lookee there! The water done froze overnight! Now, we kin walk from this island, sure as a gun has hind sights."

Jack was still groggy from his cold plunge but otherwise showed no ill effects. With Little Mink steadying him, they crossed the ice, reentered the forest, and struck off upriver until they reached a deer trail leading inland. As they trod wearily along, Little Mink reached in her pouch to find only a few crumbs of corn bread. Stopping abruptly, she said with a worried frown, "We out of food. What we do? There not much game to snare in winter."

"Why not bag a buck er doe?" suggested Jack, motioning to the fresh hoof marks stamped into the path before them.

"But have no weapon except my knife."

"Then, we'll jess have to trap 'im, girl!"

A smile crossed Little Mink's lips as she searched for a log that would serve their purpose. She settled on a beech trunk that had shattered in four pieces when felled by a windstorm. She called to Jack, and he rolled the most manageable chunk onto a shadowy stretch of the path. The girl, meanwhile, cut and notched three stout limbs that would serve as the trigger for their deadfall trap. While the woodsman tilted the log over the middle of the trail, Little Mink propped it up with the limbs that looked like the number <u>four</u> when assembled. She placed a flat rock under the vertical piece, so it didn't dig into the ground when the trap was sprung. Now, all an animal had to do was brush against the trigger to be crushed by the collapsing log.

After they had set their trap, Jack murmured, "No buck worth his salt will run into such a de-vice. We'll have to chase 'im into it."

"You right. Let's hide."

Jack and Little Mink stole fifty yards down the trail to an outcropping of rocks. They climbed up high enough so their quarry wouldn't wind them and settled in for a long wait. To pass the time, they exchanged kisses, held hands, and dreamed of sizzling hunks of venison.

Finally, as dusk spread through the forest, three doe crept stealthily down the path toward the young couple's hiding place. The lead mother moved cautiously forward sniffing for enemies. The yearlings behind her followed along in strict obedience, and Jack chuckled under his breath when he remembered how another big doe had disciplined her young by planting her hooves in the middle of the malingerers' flanks.

Hawkins and Little Mink sat frozen until the deer crept past their point of ambush. Immediately, they leaped behind the herd, waving their hands and stomping their feet. The big doe bolted forward but plunged into the brush just before reaching the trap. All legs and raised tails, the panicked youngsters fled close behind her.

In attempting to make the sharp turn, one clumsy fawn pushed the other directly into the trigger of the deadfall. A rush of wind was followed by a horrible thud and a prolonged bleat. The yearling lay trapped beneath the log, flailing its feet and calling for its mama. Little Mink rushed forward and drew her knife across the struggling deer's throat. When its life ebbed away, she rolled the deadfall off its back and slit open its belly. Jack joined her as she ripped the hot liver from the fawn's chest cavity. Slicing the liver in two, she offered half to her man before devouring her portion.

Hawkins ate hungrily, relishing each delicious bite. Finally, he mumbled, "It sure is funny how things work out. It weren't many nights ago a deadfall got me into this mess with yer people."

"You my people," corrected the girl, stroking the lightning tattoo on the back of Jack's hand.

"An' now, that same style trap jess provided the meat I need fer the journey home."

"We need."

"Yes, we need," replied Hawkins with a resigned grin. "On the way back to Ishua Town, I'll be tellin' ya all 'bout m' bad luck."

"Until I wish ears freeze shut while in river?" teased Little Mink.

"Now, ya sound like Bearbite Bob."

"That squaw chaser? Why, I even hear of him!"

"He's also a great woodsman. Right now he'd be tellin' us to clean this deer an' git movin' before the Lenni Lenape pull any more surprises."

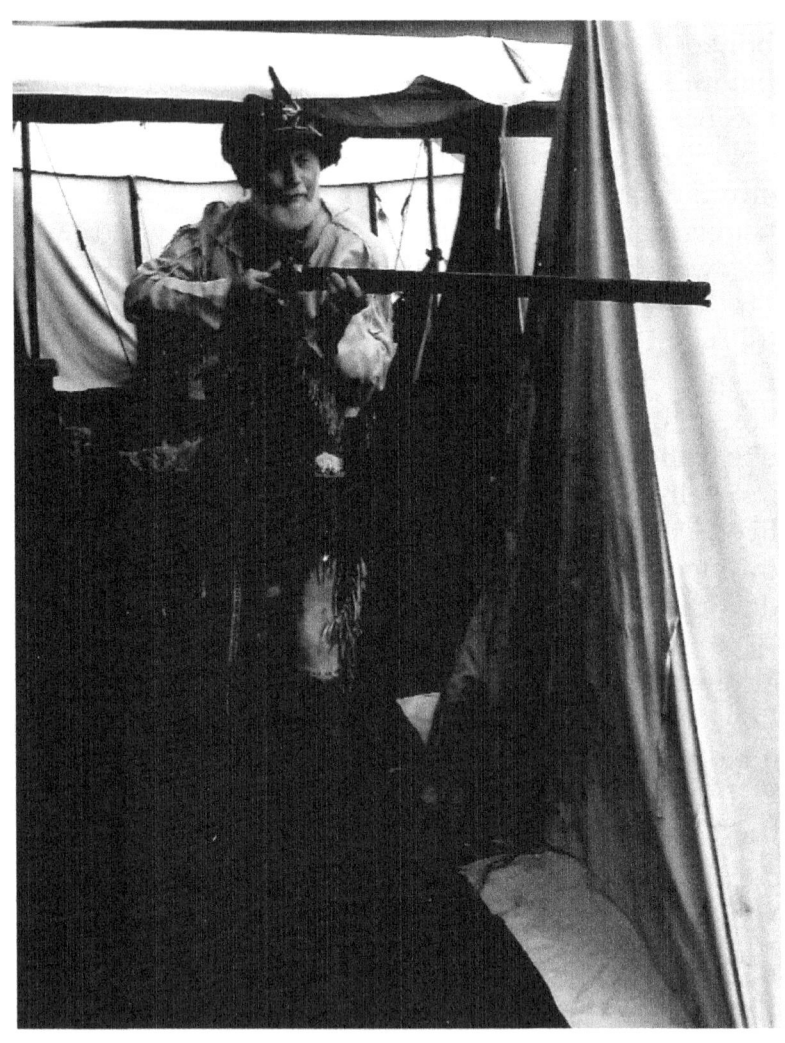

CHAPTER THIRTEEN:
A JOYFUL REUNION

Bearbite Bob peered through the swirling snow. He was standing guard outside the gates of Ishua Town with his young friend, Will Cutler. It had been a nasty night, and Bob longed for his shift to be over so he could crawl back in Bear Woman's warm bed. Despite the bitter cold, he was about to nod off when a hunter's apparition appeared suddenly out of the blizzard.

Winslow closed his eyes and then opened them again to make sure he was seeing right. The ghost had now morphed into two dim figures, and he shuddered at the eerie sight. Calling out to Will, he stammered, "D-D-Do you see somethin' comin' up the road yonder, er is m' vision p-p-playin' tricks on me?"

Cutler had been deep in thought, and worry wrinkled his otherwise boyish brow. Glancing in the direction Bob gestured to with his gun barrel, he could see nothing but wind-driven snow. Finally, when he was about to snap at the grizzled woodsman for disturbing him, Will caught a glimpse of two shadowy travelers that caused him to grumble, "Better alert the village, or go see who they are. Must be mighty weary by the way they're trudging through the drifts."

Bob cocked his flintlock and slipped ahead several paces to get a better look at the pilgrims. Suddenly, he snatched off his felt hat and waved it wildly in the air. "Glory be!" he thundered. "It's Jack Hawkins back from the grave!"

In the next instant, Winslow and Cutler bounded through the snow to catch Lightnin' and Little Mink just as they collapsed. Whooping for help, they were soon surrounded by a mob of armed braves, who lent a hand in assisting the wayfarers into their village. Bob and Will dragged Jack between them, while the girl was carried by two Iroquois who looked suspiciously at her Delaware dress. The unconscious visitors were taken to the Bear clan longhouse where Sparrow and Bright Star were already preparing pine needle tea.

The heat of the dwelling soon revived the young couple, and Bright Star wrapped bearskins around their shoulders to ease their shivering. As they sipped hot tea, Alexander MacDonald emerged from behind the curtain of a neighboring sleeping platform to vigorously shake hands with his old partner. The curtain moved again, and Mac was joined by a short, quiet woman with gentle eyes, who bent to hug Little Mink in welcome.

"Jack, I'd like ye to meet Gathering Flowers, me new wife," said MacDonald. "And who be this ye bring into our family?"

"She's Little Mink," replied Hawkins, blushing to the roots of his hair.

"Here, I thought you was a gone beaver, an' ya brung back a prime plew," cackled Bearbite, winking at the Delaware squaw.

"Me Swift Lightning's!" exclaimed Little Mink, clinging to Jack. "You stay away!"

"Then, I reckon I was right the first time," guffawed the old trapper, tugging on his long beard. "You are a gone beaver, Lightnin'!"

After the guests had drunk their fill of tea and had been served a chunk of leftover venison, Alex asked, "Where have ye been, Jack? We be worried sick about you since we found this layin' along the trail."

Pulling a long rifle from under his bed, the Scotchman handed it to Hawkins. Jack immediately leaped up to shout, "Little Lightnin'! Thanks so much fer findin' 'im! He's as much a part o' me as m' own arm!"

"While you're up, ya best tell us yer story," urged Winslow. "If ya don't, me an' Big Cat will have to go stand in the cold. Since the Delaware went on a rampage scalping every white settler in these parts, Chief Dark Thunder has us on guard every hour o' the day an' night."

"Aye, and ye can tell all the lies ye like," laughed Alex, "an' no one will contradict ya."

Hawkins grinned at the good-natured kidding. Then, he began his tale from the time he left his friends to go check their beaver traps. Especially Sparrow hung on his every word and gasped with alarm when he told of his capture and ill-treatment by the Miller brothers. Only after she heard that the hated rum traders received no payment for Jack at Kit-Han-Ne did the consternation fade from her brow.

Bright Star and Will, though, seemed preoccupied and withdrawn during Hawkins' monologue. Several times the lad tried to put his arm around his wife, only to have her scoot away. After her fifth rejection, Cutler sat sulking as black anger built up in him.

When Jack ended his yarn, Bearbite growled, "We gotta go after them Millers an' pin their ears back!"

"But they could be anywhere in this here wilderness," sighed Hawkins.

"Bob is right!" ranted Will. "We should take care of those rascals!"

"Fergit it," yawned Lightnin'. "I jess got back from that hornet's nest o' Delaware an' Frenchies. Let it be."

"Aye, give the lad a chance to catch his breath," scolded Mac. "Now, we should all go to sleep."

It was only an hour before dawn, so everyone crawled off to bed, weary yet happy that Jack had returned to them. Sparrow showed Hawkins to an empty sleeping platform where he was joined by Little Mink. Lightnin' tried to get her to go to a different bed, but she clung to him and made such a fuss that he gave up the notion.

The Bear clan slept until the dim sun of winter had completed half its journey. When they finally arose to have breakfast, Will Cutler said, "Yellow Hand told me yesterday that buffalo have yarded up not far from here. It was too close to dark for him to shoot one. You boys want to take a crack at them?"

"Do bull elk got antlers?" bellowed Bearbite.

"I'm in, too," murmured Hawkins sleepily. "You ever knowed me to turn down a huntin' trip?"

"Are ye sure you're up to it?" asked Mac with a concerned frown.

"'Course he is!" howled Bob, giving Bear Woman a sloppy kiss. "Buffalo tongue tastes almost as sweet as this girl!"

After breakfast, Jack's friends presented him with new winter clothes, while the women fussed over Little Mink and dressed her in Iroquois garb. Looking even prettier than before, she ran to Hawkins to show off her new look. When she saw him shouldering his rifle to join the other men, tears welled up in her dark eyes.

Even Hawkins was struck by Little Mink's sad beauty. After awkwardly shuffling his feet, he said, "Don't cry. I'm only goin' huntin' with my pals."

"Not want you to leave," sobbed the girl, throwing her arms around Jack's neck. "I die if you not come back!"

"Now, calm yerself, darlin'. After the way ya saved my hide, I reckon I belong to you as much as you do me. I won't be long. I promise."

Hawkins kissed Little Mink on the cheek and then gently untangled himself from her. Afterward, he slipped outside with the other hunters and pulled on the snowshoes they offered him. Without the webbed shoes, the thigh-deep snow would have been impossible to travel through for any distance. Jack knew that from the night before.

With Will leading the way, the woodsmen trudged through the thick winter hemlocks behind the village until they came to a secluded meadow piled high with drifts. On the far side, they could just see several huge brown shapes hunkered down in the snow. There were four cows and one big bull. The beasts had the whole area plowed up, so they could feed and move freely from one end to the other. Jack guessed they were eating acorns that had fallen from the oak trees bordering the field to the east.

"I'm gonna shoot me that big bull," crowed Jack, "an' make a nice sleeping robe out o' its hide. Then, maybe Little Mink will stay nice an' warm an' won't cling to me all night like wet buckskin. Do you boys know how hard it is to sleep with a girl crawlin' all over ya?"

"You should be thankful she is," grumbled Will. "Lately, Bright Star is distant as her name."

"Whooeee!" whistled Winslow. "If my squaw was crawlin' all over me, I wouldn't worry 'bout sleepin'!"

"Hey, Little Mink ain't my squaw," protested Hawkins. "We ain't married, er nothin'."

"Well, you best git to it then," chortled Bearbite, "'cause the way you're goin', it won't be long afore a youngin's wearin' yer face."

"Enough o' this talk," chastised Mac. "Are ye going to shoot those bison or chase 'em around in the dark?"

The other hunters grinned sheepishly and then followed MacDonald to the edge of the meadow. The frigid buffalo were bedded down and paid no attention to them at all. After slipping off his snowshoes, Lightnin' said, "I'm gonna git nose-to-nose with that big bull before I shoots him. That way I kin be sure o' hittin' 'im in the head an' not damage that fine hide."

"Do ye know how mean those brutes be?" warned Alex. "Ye can always sew up a bullet hole if your hands aren't useless from a tramplin'."

"Okay, Ma MacDonald," scoffed Jack. "An' if I play with bows an' arrows, I'll put out my eye. Watch an' learn how a real man kills a buffalo."

Jack entered the trampled part of the field and walked boldly to within fifty yards of the huge bull. When he came to a halt, the bison rose snorting to its six foot height and glared at the hunter with fearless eyes. It began stomping its hooves and blowing steam out its black, round nostrils as Jack cocked his long rifle, took steady aim, and carefully squeezed the trigger.

Instead of the usual roar that accompanied a falling hammer, there was just a loud click. Too late, Jack realized that he had forgotten to prime his pan. When he looked up again, he found himself facing a shaggy ton of irate male buffalo itching to protect its mates. The bull pawed the snow twice more and then broke into a trot toward Hawkins. It had only gone a few more feet before it reached full velocity. Lightnin' stared transfixed at the oncoming horns that twisted to impale him. The breath of the beast was upon him before instinct took over. Finally, with an alarmed yelp, Jack dove away from the swaying black head and deadly, stomping hooves.

The buffalo whirled with surprising agility and charged Hawkins a second time. Not wanting to outmaneuver the rushing bull, Jack sprang to his feet and raced full speed across the flattened snow. Unfortunately, he was so worried about the brute closing fast behind him that he dashed straight toward the cows. Only the snorts of the herd alerted him in time, and he veered off just as they, too, stampeded to crush him.

Now, the field was alive with rumbling motion as the bison galloped to and fro after the two-legged intruder. Jack dodged and weaved and weaved and juked until his legs turned to rubber. Nearly winded, he made for a tall oak and clambered up it like a monkey. The riled beasts continued to mill about sniffing the air and bellowing with rage.

The tree Jack climbed was slippery with ice, and the bull began to bang against it to dislodge the hunter. Vibrations shook the trunk until Hawkins felt his grip weaken. Just when he began to slip, a shot rang out. As his tormentor crashed to the ground at the base of the oak, the cows thundered into the woods. Afterward, all was quiet until Will, Bob, and Alex came stamping through the dusk on their snowshoes.

"You can come down now," called Cutler, after stifling a loud laugh.

"An' here I thought you was a stander," chortled Bearbite, "'til I seen ya flee from that big bull."

"Aye, it seems we always find ye up a stump," added Mac with a merry twinkle in his eyes. "Too bad Young Jacobs weren't here. Ye could have climbed him to safety."

"Funnnny!" wheezed Hawkins, scrambling down from his perch. "You didn't hit 'im in the hump, an' ruin that robe I be needin'?"

"You should be happy I hit 'im at all," teased Winslow, "afore he jarred ya out o' that oak."

"But what about the robe?"

"Oh, don't worry," snickered Mac, "Ye'll be getting it soon enough as a wedding gift from me an' the boys."

CHAPTER FOURTEEN: SPRING AT LAST

The winter was unusually harsh, and Ishua Town held a boisterous celebration when the ice finally melted from the Allegheny. The festivities began with Jack and Little Mink donning rabbit skin clothes to be wed in the Iroquois tradition. Bearbite Bob and Bear Woman surprised everyone when they became one at the same ceremony. Winslow looked quite pale in his wedding garb, for his bride kept jabbing him in the back with a concealed dagger until Chief Dark Thunder proclaimed them man and wife.

When planting month arrived, Hawkins' new wife rushed to him one morning with joy spilling from her eyes. "I was asked to help Society of Women Planters," she chimed. "Now, I full member of Iroquois!"

"That's fine as frog's fur," beamed Hawkins, squeezing her soft hand, "but I reckon you was always accepted by the way them women fussed over ya the night we stumbled out o' the blizzard."

"I go now. Sparrow's calling me."

"Then, you best run along. Me an' Will is gonna play us some checkers to pass the time."

Little Mink scurried to the far end of the Bear clan longhouse where the wives were preparing the seed corn for planting. Bear Woman, Gathering Flowers, and several of their friends were prying the fattest, best shaped kernels from the center of some ears of corn, while Sparrow and Bright Star brewed a strong herbal tea from a secret recipe. The select kernels were then placed in wooden bowls and the tea poured over them. When the process was completed, Little Mink asked, "How long will corn need to soak before we plant it?"

"Seven nights," replied Sparrow. "Kernels must soften in potion that fend off crows and bugs. Now, we burn tobacco and pray: Tharonhiawakon, Holder of the Heavens, hear the words of the people here assembled. The smoke of tobacco rises. Give attention to our words as they rise to you in this smoke. We thank you for the return of this season of planting. Grant us a good season so that our harvest will be great."

A week later, after breakfast, Sparrow and the Bear clan women scooped the seed corn into their aprons and stepped out the longhouse door to join the other girls, mothers, and grandmothers from the rest of the village. As they marched solemnly toward the distant fields, Sparrow handed Little Mink a highly decorated container made of bark. "Here, you carry spirit of Onenhste, the Corn Maiden. She must be with us to ensure success."

"I'm honored," murmured Little Mink. "Thank you."

When the women caught sight of the fields ahead, they began a singsong chant praising the fruits of the earth. The clearing contained rows of dirt mounds piled calf-high. These hills were built between the blackened skeletons of trees that the men girdled the spring before and then burned in the fall to provide fertilizing ash for the soil.

The women spread out to place seven corn seeds in the top of each hill. After they'd planted just two rows in the Bear clan field, Sparrow shooed them into the Wolf clan corn patch to plant two rows. As they whisked toward the

Turtle clan mounds, Little Mink inquired, "Why do we move around so? Would it not be easier to plant whole field before going to next?"

"Are you a fool?" snapped Bright Star. "What if storm come? Then, one clan get no seed in ground. Harmony broken among Society of Women Planters."

"I'm sorry. I not think."

"I'm sorry, too," choked the princess after an embarrassed silence. "I mad at husband. Take it out on you."

Little Mink flashed Bright Star a forgiving smile and then asked, "When do we plant squash and beans? And why are they sisters to corn?"

"Three crops help each other through growing season," explained Sparrow, who had edged closer after Bright Star's outburst. "Bean Sister grow tall by twining up Corn Maiden. Squash Sister spread out at their feet to keep ground damp and choke weeds. Oak leaves must be full grown before plant other sisters, not size of squirrel's ear like today."

While the women were tending to the fields, the men of the village assembled on the banks of the Allegheny for some spring fishing. Bored with their game of checkers, Will and Jack tagged along to get some needed exercise.

Dark Thunder was directing the activity when the woodsmen arrived on the riverbank. They watched fascinated as braves drove poles into the stream bottom to create a v-shape barrier. The widest part of this fish trap was at the head of a long pool and then converged into a small opening leading to the rapids above.

Hawkins and Cutler were handed spears and told to wade into the river and stand where the barrier narrowed. After they were joined by several other fishermen, Dark Thunder ordered the remaining braves to attach a large rake behind a pair of powerful black mares. The horses were led into the riffles at the bottom of the river pool and urged upstream by their drivers. The rake churned behind them as the mares splashed with pumping legs and whinnies of protest toward the waiting fish hunters above.

When the horses plunged into deeper water above the riffles, a steady stream of bass, pickerel, and white fish was funneled into the v-shaped trap. While Jack struck futilely at a thirty inch pickerel snaking past his knee, Will gasped at the sight of a squash-sized smallmouth. It didn't take Cutler long, however, to recover from his surprise. Spying another mammoth bass, he drove the point of his weapon deep into its back. "Got to lead them," he squawked to Hawkins, "just like you would a running deer."

"My reflexes ain't as fast as yourn," retorted Jack. "I reckon they're even quicker this mornin' after that row you had with Bright Star."

"Don't want to talk about it!" growled Will, viciously gaffing a second fish.

"Well, ya best do somethin' afore ya lose her."

"And you should pay attention to where you're poking that spear before you drive it through somebody's leg!"

Reddening at Will's rebuke, Lightnin' struck again and again but could not hit his darting quarry no matter how large they were. After missing a four-foot sturgeon, he shook his head in disgust and splashed ashore to escape the freezing river.

The Iroquois fishermen, though, seemed oblivious to the cold current. They were too busy sticking one pickerel after another to worry about the numbness of their legs. They dropped their squirming catch into baskets held by small boys and then poised over the water to impale another fish. Will was equally focused and proficient with his spear while he concentrated on the bass.

    Being useless as a fish hunter, Hawkins stayed ashore to help clean the braves' take. He dreamed of Little Mink, too, as he watched some busy lads build fires over which to smoke the bass and pickerel. This had become a lazy day, and he grinned when the May sun broke through the clouds to drive the chill from his long shanks. He couldn't remember when he was happier. He only wished that his wife would return from the fields, for he suddenly missed her loving touch.

CHAPTER FIFTEEN: BURIAL RITES

After the Iroquois women finished planting the seed corn, they trudged from the fields toward the distant village. The sun beat fiercely from the afternoon sky until Sparrow stopped to mop her brow. Finally, she said in a hoarse whisper to Bright Star, Little Mink, and Bear Woman, "There's a spring nearby. Why not stop for drink?"

Exchanging weary smiles, the women followed their clan mother down a slick embankment encumbered with brush. At the bottom, they found a clear-running stream gushing from beneath a large rock. Bending in turn, they greedily slurped water until their thirst was sated. Then, they lounged in the shade and rested their eyes from the blinding glare of the spring woods.

Little Mink stood up to stretch her cramped muscles and found herself surrounded by a patch of blooming pussy willows. Giggling with delight, she scrambled to pick some furry catkins. She had barely gathered a small handful when a large, dirty paw stretched from the thicket to latch hold of her.

Little Mink gasped in surprise and pulled back hard until she broke free. Curses immediately erupted from the dense shrubs as Randall Miller, the filthy rum trader, lunged forward to secure the girl in his burly arms. Little Mink squealed directly into her attacker's ear, and he stumbled backward with a disoriented grunt. Slipping in the overflow from the spring, he toppled heavily onto his back with the maiden scratching for his eyes.

It was then that Rupert Miller stepped from the brush brandishing a blunderbuss pistol. Pointing the flared muzzle at the other three women, he snarled, "Don't even think o' helpin' yer friend. Randall, quit playin' with that squaw, an' fetch her here."

But Randall was beset by a wildcat who continued to rake him with her nails and shriek into his punctured eardrum. In desperation, he grabbed Little Mink roughly by the hair and flung her off. Struggling to his feet, he assailed her with a torrent of heavy kicks until Sparrow leaped on his back and bit him viciously on his good ear.

Randall spun around and around like a man fighting off a swarm of bees. Finally, his brother lurched forward to bring the heavy barrel of his pistol down on Sparrow's skull. As the clan mother slid senseless to the ground, the villain barked, "Enough o' this nonsense. We're the ones with weapons, an' you're gonna do what we say."

"That's right!" bellowed Randall, favoring his gnawed ear. "We come back to exact our revenge on them men of yers. What better way than to have our way with you."

"You not only ones that armed," screeched Bear Woman, pulling a dagger from beneath her deerskin skirt.

"Yes!" cried Little Mink, springing up to yank out a flint knife. "Now, no one touch me!"

"A knife ag'in a pistol?" jeered Rupert. "You won't make it two steps afore I drill ya through the heart."

"You shoot this close to village," warned Bright Star, "and braves come from all directions to carve out your liver and feed it to dogs!"

A fearful look passed briefly through Rupert's eyes before they hardened again. "By then, we'll have had what we want from you an' be long gone," he cackled.

"Not from me!" shrieked Bear Woman, rushing the gunman with her upraised dagger.

Rupert whirled, and the willow grove exploded with the roar of his pistol. A huge hole appeared in the left side of Bear Woman's chest, and she was hurled violently backward. She had no sooner landed in a wasted heap when Bright Star snatched up her fallen sister's dagger and plunged it deep in the rum trader's ribs.

Regaining consciousness, Sparrow then flung herself around Randall's legs. Unable to move, he became an easy target for Little Mink, who slashed her knife across his jaw, cutting him to the bone.

Rupert, meanwhile, yanked the dagger from his seeping wound and cuffed Bright Star with a backhand to her pretty face. This only incensed the princess further, and she answered with a kick to the brawler's crotch. Whimpering in pain, the burly man withered to the ground. The girl then snatched up a rock and pulverized his nose with it. Over and over she bashed him, not caring that she was covered with his blood. She continued her wild assault even after his soul departed for hell.

Randall was in too much trouble to help his brother. After kicking Sparrow free, he still couldn't dodge past Little Mink, who lunged at him from every possible angle. Grabbing a dead limb, he swung at her viciously, only to slip on the wet ground and fall facedown in the mud. Before he could rise to defend himself, the enraged girl grabbed him by his greasy hair and ran her knife across the pig bristles sprouting on his throat. Blood gushed from the wide wound, and Randall fought no more.

By the time Dark Thunder led a whooping band of warriors to the scene, the women were gathered over Bear Woman to mourn her death. Their keening also brought Lightnin', Bearbite, Mac, and Will scrambling from the village with their long rifles.

When Winslow saw his wife lying in a pool of her own blood, he dropped to his knees beside her. With tears streaming into his beard, he croaked, "Wall now, ain't that dandy? I finally finds a squaw to tame me, an' the Great Spirit takes her away. I'll never fergit ya, Bear Woman. Not as long as there's fish swimmin' in the rivers an' beaver buildin' lodges. Ain't no one can take yer place in my heart."

Seeing Little Mink and Bright Star splattered with gore, their husbands rushed to comfort them. "Are you all right?" gasped Lightnin', catching his wife in his arms.

"Me fine now that you're here," whispered Little Mink, returning Jack's embrace.

"And how are you?" asked Will as he attempted to hug his Iroquois princess.

"Good!" snapped Bright Star, pushing him away. "Only wish we not kill bad men. Then, Father burn them slow like they deserve!"

"Already got what deserve!" cried Sparrow, wiping blood from the corner of her mouth. "Their evil brought much sorrow to our people."

Four braves wrapped Bear Woman's lifeless body in a blanket and picked it up between them. As the mourners solemnly marched off to Ishua Town, Alexander gestured toward the Miller brothers' rent corpses and asked, "What about these rascals?"

"Let the crows eat them," grunted Dark Thunder.

The Iroquois carried Bear Woman back to the Bear clan longhouse where Sparrow and a tearful Gathering Flowers washed her fatal wound and dressed her in the finest deerskin garments. After elaborately painting Bear Woman's face, the others gathered items from her everyday life to bury with her. They set her kettle, wooden spoons, pottery, and glass beads beside her body. When they brought out dried fish, pemmican, and tobacco, a somber Winslow murmured, "What's the food fer, Sparrow? My poor wife ain't gonna eat no more."

"Bear Woman now depart on road for heaven. It long and winding and take whole year to travel. Must have food, or her spirit perish."

The Bear clan women had just finished preparations for the funeral when a delegation from the tribe entered the longhouse. Standing before the hearth, the head elder produced strands of mourning wampum from a pouch and handed them to Bob Winslow. Afterward, he said to Bearbite, "We here on behalf of whole people to express our sorrow. May the Great Spirit comfort thee in thy sadness."

Just before sundown, men from the Bear clan wrapped Bear Woman in a shroud and bore her to a circular grave outside the village. The burial pit had been lined with only the softest bearskin, and the corpse was eased into a sitting position before being lowered into its final resting place. As two braves faced Bear Woman to the east, Gathering Flowers passed down her dead cousin's personal effects and food provisions into the grave.

Renewed wailing accompanied the interment. Then, a bereaved Sparrow sobbed, "Oh, Bear Woman, listen once more to words of your clan mother. You have departed from us, and our wise and great Creator ordered it thus. By His will we left to taste more miseries of this world. Thy husband, friends, and relations have gathered to look upon thee for last time. They, mourn, as with one mind, thy departure from us. Our Maker has called thee home. We follow soon to be parted from thee no more."

Bearbite Bob was too choked up to add to the funeral address. His face was pale beneath his beard, and Alexander, Will, and Jack took turns supporting him as he suffered through the ceremony on wobbly knees.

As the sun set to leave a bloody streak across the horizon, Little Mink freed a captured bird over the grave. "Bear away our sister's spirit," she sniffed as the bird sped off. "Take her to her heavenly rest."

On the other side of the village crows squawked and cawed as they swooped down to join an unholy feast with buzzards. Sharp beaks tore flesh and plucked out dead eyeballs. There'd be nothing left for the dogs to gnaw on but bones.

CHAPTER SIXTEEN: MORE DANGER

After his wife's murder, Bearbite Bob spent endless days slumped in front of the Bear clan longhouse. Sometimes he whittled, but mostly he stared toward the far horizon. He refused to eat, too, while visiting the place that only true mourners ever seek.

Finally, one sultry morning in late May, Jack Hawkins shook Winslow by the shoulder and blared, "Wall now, you're jess the fella I've been lookin' fer to go explorin' down Susquehanna way. Game's mighty scarce in these parts, and we's all gettin' soft hangin' 'round this here village. Will's up fer it. An' even Mac's goin'. What do ya say? Better stir from there afore ya grow roots an' sprout into a big old thorn tree!"

A brief smile flickered through Bob's beard, and the distance faded from his eyes. He coughed a couple of times and then wheezed, "I reckon you're right, Lightnin'. Help me up, will ya, an' I'll go git packed."

"No need, old man. Yer gear's already in my canoe."

"Who you callin' old? Why, I kin still see a buck's eye at two hundred yards an' a bear's at three."

"But do ya got enough spring in them legs ta carry ya down to the river?"

"Yes, an' plenty to kick yer rear, too!"

As Jack pulled Bearbite to his feet, Will streaked out of the longhouse with Bright Star in hot pursuit. Smacking him with a wooden spoon, she fumed, "You leave here, and you not welcome back! No place in heart for man who wanders."

"What heart?" cried Will, wheeling to face the princess. "I don't think ya have one!"

"Come on, Big Cat," said Jack, hustling his friend down to the Allegheny. "Let her simmer in her own juice fer a while, an' she'll be done fightin' ya. You'll see."

Mac stood on the riverbank hugging Gathering Flowers goodbye. Little Mink was also waiting there to embrace Hawkins. "I know you go to help friend through sadness," she whispered tearfully. "Come back to me soon."

"I will," choked Jack, reluctantly tearing himself away from her. "An' I'll bring ya a nice gift."

Bearbite was already in the stern of the second elm bark canoe when Lightnin' climbed in the front and snatched up his paddle. He dared not look back at his wife when they cast off to follow Will and Mac's craft upstream. The Allegheny was running full from the spring rains, and the travelers had to work hard to make progress against the strong current. They dug their paddles deep into the swift water and only pressed on for two hours before their aching arms forced them to draw up on a sandbar.

Even with frequent stops, Hawkins and his friends made good time. By late afternoon, they reached the confluence of the stream they'd been seeking. Here, they built a small campfire and cooked the bass Lightnin' caught before dark using a hand line and a bird's claw hook.

"The Delaware's way o' fishin' beats spearin' 'em all ta hell!" Jack crowed to Cutler as they munched on crispy filets. "Don't ruin no meat, neither."

"You old fellows need some way to catch bass," teased Will, shaking his shock of blonde hair. "Especially when your reflexes go."

"I'm only in m' twenties. Don't tell me that 'til I'm Bearbite's age."

"Why, I kin still outfight, outhunt, an' outshoot any o' you whippersnappers," growled Bob. "On any day o' the week!"

"That's the Bearbite we know," chortled Hawkins, slapping his pal on the shoulder. "Welcome back!"

The travelers woke at daylight and set off for another difficult day of paddling. The smaller stream they entered was filled with snags that kept them vigilant as they slipped along. Often, they had to abandon their canoes and carry them around rapids too shallow to allow passage. After the fifth time they had done this, Bearbite flew into a rage as he helped Jack lug their craft over slippery, shin-bruising rocks.

"Now, I know why they named this stinkin' run 'Portage Creek!' " roared Bob after filling the air with curses.

"Hey, at least it rid ya o' the anger you was carryin'," snickered Lightnin'.

By noon the travelers had run out of deep water altogether, so they hid their canoes in a brush pile and continued along on foot. It took them the rest of the day to tramp to the head of the valley. When they finally made camp atop the divide leading to the Susquehanna River, sleep found them as soon as they wrapped themselves in their blankets.

The next morning the woodsmen took a more leisurely pace to gawk at the wildly beautiful land that spread before them. Creeping down a well-marked trail, they gaped at the round-topped gobblers knobs that dominated the valley. The hillsides rose to incredible heights around them and abounded with house-sized rocks and huge groves of virgin pine. Tangled masses of blossoming laurel filled the air with sweetness, and a carpet of wildflowers added splashes of violet, pink, and yellow to nature's palette.

Will was so enthralled with the Susquehanna country that he rambled ahead of his friends to fully enjoy the splendor that surrounded him. His eyes focused on everything but the trail, and only a sharp buzz kept him from stepping on a four-foot timber rattler that had crawled out on the sun-drenched path to warm itself. The snake had now coiled into a striking position, and its head weaved menacingly back-and-forth waiting for Will to flinch.

Cutler couldn't back away, so he stood sweating until Jack stole up behind him. "Looks like you're in a fix," murmured Hawkins. "Jess stay froze there 'til I take care o' that rascal."

Lightnin' inched into the brush, picked up a long limb, and broke the branches from it. Afterward, he slipped back onto the trail and crept to the right of the rattler. He shook his stick and hissed loudly until the snake squirmed to face him. His diversion allowed Will to leap from danger.

Before Jack could whack the serpent, its diamond-shaped head snapped forward to strike the air inches from his leg. Leaping backward in surprise, Hawkins swung wildly, and the branch flew from his shaking hands. In an instant the snake recoiled for a second strike. Just as the deadly head reared back to gain momentum, Will crushed it beneath a rock he hurled with accuracy and ire.

"Why didn't you just shoot the damn snake?" yelped Will when Jack strode forward to shake his hand.

"An' alert every hostile within twenty miles? I'd rather take m' chances with the rattler."

"And a fine, long fellow he be, too!" exclaimed Mac, bending to cut off the venomous head. "There's enough meat here to feed Ishua Town."

The woodsmen walked only a short distance farther before they came to a waterfall tumbling down over the mountain to form a spring pool. It was such a scenic place that they set up camp there. While Will gathered wood for a fire, Mac skinned the rattlesnake and washed its flesh. There was a thunderstorm brewing, too, so Jack and Bearbite started work on a temporary shelter built of canvas and tree limbs.

Soon, the friends were gathered around a crackling fire roasting hunks of snake meat on spits. "Tastes jess like frog legs, don't it?" chortled Bob, wiping snake juice from his beard.

"An' here I thought you was gonna say 'chicken,' like ya did when we et that turtle a while back," joshed Lightnin'. "Where's yer appetite, Will?"

"This rattler reminds me too much of my wife for it to taste good," grumped Cutler.

"Ah, Bright Star ain't that bad," quipped Winslow. "She jess don't like ya strayin' too far from her snake den. Eat up, now, afore yer meat gits cold."

"No, you can have my share. I'll go down to the creek yonder and finger out a few trout from under the bank."

"Rattlers like it down there, too," said Jack with a mischievous grin.

"Then, I'll wait for breakfast," croaked Will. "That is if the rain in those clouds overhead doesn't wash us down the mountainside!"

CHAPTER SEVENTEEN: THE BLAZE

Will's prediction about the severity of the storm proved true. He no sooner finished speaking when rain fell in sheets and sent the woodsmen scrambling for their makeshift shelter. Immediately after, the wind howled from the dark trees to rock the hut and rip the branches from its fragile sides. When the canvas roof lifted and blew away, Cutler and his pals skedaddled for the nearest hemlock thicket. Hailstones sped them on their mad flight, smacking their skin and fueling their curses.

Morning found the friends huddled around a smoky fire. They sat shivering in wet blankets, rubbing their cramped muscles and staring dull-eyed at the dripping woods. Finally, their trembling became so violent that they shouldered their rifles and stomped off down the steep trail to quell the chills that racked them.

The hikers slopped along in a cold drizzle until the valley widened at the confluence of a larger stream that flowed in from the west. Here, Hawkins said, "If I remember right, some folks built a fort not far from here. Inside them walls, four families share a nice cabin."

"Sure hope they got a fire roarin' up their chimney," muttered Bob through chattering teeth.

"And a fine breakfast of oatmeal cooking over it," added Cutler.

"Next, ye'll be wishin' for a saucy maid to serve it to ye," grunted Mac. "I wish I'd never left me bonnie wife to come on such a journey."

Thoughts of a warm cabin quickened the woodsmen's pace, and they strode with renewed purpose through the drenched countryside. They hadn't tramped more than a mile farther downstream when they saw smoke rising beyond an orchard just ahead.

"Wagh! Is that a sight fer sore eyes!" exclaimed Winslow. "Won't be long afore the steam will be risin' from these buckskins, an' I'll be drinkin' hot rum as fast as they kin fetch it."

"Don't that look like a powerful lot o' smoke to be pourin' out a chimney?" asked Lightnin'.

"Ye be right," groaned Mac. "The whole place is on fire!"

The hunters primed their long rifles with dry powder and then tore off toward the burning stockade. Before they reached it, they saw fresh moccasin tracks that caused them to scramble for cover in the orchard. They had just ducked behind trees when a band of Delaware led by King Beaver emerged from the billowing smoke dragging a woman captive and her two small children.

Peeking out from behind a tree trunk, Hawkins saw the warriors tie the writhing woman to the fort gate. The braves had black masks painted on their faces and howled with such frenzy that Lightnin' swore they were drunk or mad. The Indians were still out of rifle range, so Jack listened helplessly as the screaming mother wailed, "No. No. Please, no!"

It was then that King Beaver grabbed one of her little boys by the legs and dashed out his brains on the stockade wall. A second warrior threw down her other son and severed his neck with one hack of his razor-sharp hatchet. The death of her children pushed the woman's shrieks to ear-piercing decibels until King Beaver sunk his ax in her skull to silence her.

(Photo courtesy of Randy Quinn)

As more captives were driven from the flaming cabin, Jack glanced at Will and saw that his face had gone white. Even Mac, who'd witnessed such atrocities at the Battle of Culloden, sat gaping in wide-eyed horror. Bearbite, however, seethed with anger. Cocking the hammer of his long rifle, he leaped suddenly to his feet and bolted toward the carnage. His friends had no choice, then, but to follow him, and they swooped like avenging angels down on the unsuspecting Delaware.

The Indians were so intent on ripping the scalps from the dead woman and her children that they didn't notice the woodsmen until Jack's patched ball struck one of the murderers through the temple. King Beaver immediately sprang to his feet to emit a blood-curdling whoop. Spying the charging Winslow through the smoke, the chief flung his hatchet with all his might. The weapon sang off the old trapper's gunstock, nicking his bicep. Bob yelped in pain and then fired from the hip at the nearest Delaware. The painted fiend was blown sideways as hot lead ripped through him.

King Beaver whooped again, and the burning stockade fairly vomited Indians. Will and Mac fired into the throng, knocking two more braves from their feet. Jack and Bearbite, meanwhile, bashed away with their rifle butts at a swarm of looters whose arms were full of stolen food and muskets. This show of sudden force and ferocity caused the Delaware to flee into the forest, dragging several young girls behind them.

With his face flushed with rage and battle lust, Bearbite reloaded his gun and charged after the retreating war party. He had only run a few yards into the brush when the whine of bullets sent him flying on his face. Peering over a log, he saw a line of braves strung out to cover King Beaver's retreat. For five full minutes they laid down an unrelenting barrage until, yipping like wolves, they cut and ran before Bob could get off a shot.

"It's a good thing surprise be in our favor, or our scalps would be hangin' off some brave's belt," choked Mac when Winslow returned to the flaming stockade.

"I-I-I don't think they knew how many of us there were," stammered the sweating Cutler.

"Too bad we didn't git here sooner," bemoaned Bob. "We wasn't able to save any lives, an' them devils took the youngins."

Nodding solemnly at Bearbite's words, Jack turned to watch the remains of the fort collapse in heaps of cinders and scorched timber. Sifting through the smoldering ruins, they soon discovered the charred bodies of two men and a woman. Another male corpse, untouched by fire, lay face up with two tomahawks lodged in its skull.

As the woodsmen began digging shallow graves, they heard the clopping of hooves echo from down the valley. In the next instant, a pale settler came galloping toward them waving a pistol in his hand. "Who are you men?" he demanded while grimly surveying the wreckage.

"We's the ones who drove off King Beaver an' his fiends," replied Hawkins evenly. "Sure wish you'd been here to help us fight."

"I would have if my mare hadn't throwed me a mile back. She got frightened by a bear that crossed our trail an' run off. I chased her around the woods for an hour afore I caught her."

"Then, ye be lucky she bolted, or ye be lyin' next to these poor folks," croaked Mac, gesturing toward the long row of corpses that now included the tortured woman and her two sons.

"W-W-Why, that's me wife, Hannah!" cried the settler, scrambling down from his horse to kneel beside the dead woman. "They even k-k-k-killed my wee boys!"

"An' the rest o' the children they dragged off," said Alex sadly.

"At least you stopped these four!" snarled the man, nodding to the braves gunned down by the woodsmen. "Why haven't you scalped the dogs yet? You know there's a bounty on them, don't ya?"

"A bounty?" echoed Bob with a callous gleam in his eye.

"That's right! Pennsylvania declared war on the rascals at Carlisle. For every male prisoner brung in, they pays a hundred fifty Spanish dollars. For every male scalp, it's one hundred thirty dollars. Delaware women an' children earns ya money, too, dead or alive."

"Wall now, ain't that interestin'!" exclaimed Bearbite. "If we can't trap beaver, might as well ketch us some two-legged varmints."

"Aye, but the two-legged ones shoot back," reminded Alexander.

"That shouldn't bother you," grunted the settler. "With your sand, you should join the rangers."

"Why the rangers?" asked Winslow.

"'Cause them boys scout the woods an' let folks know before the Delaware attack them. They're paid by Pennsylvania, so you'd get a wage for helpin'."

"Let me git this straight," cackled Bearbite. "Jess fer joinin' these rangers we'd git paid, and on top o that we'd make a hundred plus dollars fer every scalp er Injun we brung in."

"That's right," sniffed the man before breaking down to sob over his wife's body.

"Wall, what do ya say, boys?" asked Bob. "Let's sign up with that ranger outfit. Might as well git somethin' out o' this war we's trapped in."

"I'm with you, Bearbite!" exclaimed Will. "I like the idea of helping our settlers. No use returning to Ishua Town, anyhow, with the way Bright Star treats me. What about you, Jack?"

"It sure tore at my heartstrings seein' these folks butchered. I hate to be away from Little Mink, but I reckon if someone don't stop these Delaware, they'll be knockin' at our door next jess like them Miller varmints done."

"Aye, ye be right," sighed Mac, "but I come to America to escape bloodshed. Good luck to ye lads. I'll be headin' home to me darlin' wife."

"Where do we find the rangers?" wondered Will.

"At Fort Granville," declared the settler. "An' I want you to shoot plenty of them red devils for what they done to my poor Thaddeus, Jonah, an' Matty."

"What about you?" inquired Hawkins kindly. "What are yer plans?"

"To head for Philadelphia where it's safe. Hey, you still ain't ripped the scalps from them savages that m-m-murdered my family."

"Be my guest," murmured Alex. "I'll not have their blood on me hands."

"Me neither," agreed Jack. "I could use them Spanish dollars to buy Little Mink a nice gift, but I'll not git 'em that way."

"What are ya? Snowflakes. Stand aside an' I'll take care o' it," growled Bearbite. "We'll need travelin' money if we's joinin' the rangers. Ya fergit about that?"

"But how about this poor husband?" asked Will. "We should give him some money for a new start."

"All right," droned Bob as he drew his knife. "I'll hack the hair from this here brave jess fer him."

CHAPTER EIGHTEEN: ANOTHER LONG JOURNEY

After Will, Bob, Jack, and Alex finished burying the dead at the destroyed stockade, the grieving husband led them down to the river. "You men can have my canoe for your trip to Fort Granville," he choked. "With luck, this old mare will get me far away from this place."

Without waiting for the woodsmen to even thank him, the settler leaped on his horse and galloped off to the east. After he had gone, Mac said, "I best be headin' out, too. I got a long walk ahead o' me."

"Watch yer topknot," warned Jack, shaking his friend's hand. "Give Little Mink a hug fer me."

"Have a safe trip," added Will. "I'd ask you to hug Bright Star, but what's the use? She'd just push you away."

"Don't give up, laddie. Some time apart can't hurt ye. Farewell, Bob. Take care o' that scraggly hide o' yours."

"It's them Delaware ya best be worried 'bout," chuckled Bearbite. "I'm gonna collect so many scalps, there won't be enough savages left fer a war party!"

Cutler, Winslow, and Hawkins waved goodbye to Mac. Then, they scrambled into the settler's long canoe and embarked down the swirling river. The West Branch of the Susquehanna was narrow here and filled with rocks and snags. Jack sat in the bow to thwart these obstructions, while Bearbite steered from the stern. Will did more daydreaming than paddling from his place in the midsection of the canoe and gazed in awe at the hemlock-choked crags that rose to prodigious heights around them. There were deer feeding on the riverbanks to contemplate, too, and Cutler wondered at how red their summer coats looked. An occasional swimming beaver brought a frown to the lad's face as he thought about how this war with the Delaware had ruined his livelihood.

The river stayed small and dangerous until a large feeder stream flowed in from the right. Then, it only took minimal paddling to keep the craft going at a steady pace. Staying in the middle of the current, the woodmen traveled all the way to the confluence with the east branch of the river in one day.

The following morning, the travelers found themselves on a monster of a waterway filled with dangerous eddies, huge boulders, and islands bordered by canoe-busting rocks. Now, even Will had to watch for oncoming perils. To heighten their uneasiness, they passed several rafts filled with wild-eyed settlers fleeing downriver. Bawling goats, squealing pigs, and crates of squawking chickens were packed in between spinning looms and barrels of flour. Silent children sat atop hastily packed clothes chests bursting with flapping shirt sleeves and pants legs. Mothers knelt praying, while fathers sat grimly gripping muskets. No one answered Will's waves or Jack's shouts of encouragement.

"Them settlers act like they's dead already," remarked Bearbite, spitting tobacco juice into the river. "If ya don't stay an' fight fer what's yers, ya might as well turn yer toes up."

As the woodsmen floated past the mouth of Penn's Creek, Jack said, "Used to be a fine little Dutch town up that brook. Mac an' me stopped fer supplies there when we first come to this neck o' the woods. It musta got burned out, 'cause I seen a couple o' their girls at Kit-Han-Ne. They was held by the Hickman clan, so I never could talk to 'em to find out what happened."

"I heared them folks was the first to feel the Delaware hatchets," confirmed Winslow. "Had no warnin' er the brass to fight back."

"After living among friendly Indians, the attack was probably a real shock to those Dutch," suggested Will. "It didn't mean they weren't brave."

"Then, how do ya ex-plain the scared looks on them faces we jess passed?" grunted Bearbite. "Ya either fight er die in this here country."

Winslow and his friends continued downstream until they reached the junction of the Susquehanna with another broad river dumping into it. "Up yonder's Fort Granville," said Hawkins, pointing to the right.

"What do they call that river?" asked Will.

"The Juniata."

The hunters steered into the mouth of the Juniata and found the water murky and high. "Must have been a thunderstorm upstream," observed Cutler upon noting the dark silt.

"Er a sign we's headed fer trouble," contended Bearbite. "Better keep our eyes peeled jess in case."

As Bob and Jack paddled noiselessly past an island jutting from the left side of the stream, Will primed his long rifle and scanned the woods with trepidation. It was ominously quiet here with no songbirds filling the air with their usual gaiety. The shadows intermingled with patches of sunlight to create a dizzying maze. As they drew even with the inlet, Cutler suddenly cocked his piece and aimed intently along its barrel. Luckily what he mistook for movement was just the sun glinting off a spider web.

"This place gives me the shakes," muttered Will, gripping his firearm with sweaty palms.

"Mac didn't take to it much neither," whispered Hawkins, "when we explored this river in the spring o' '50 er so. We was gonna have supper here 'til we dug a fire pit an' found busted bones an' skulls all dumped together like. Considerin' the arrowheads buried with 'em, there must have been some Injun battle on that island."

"Then, let's git," urged Bearbite, digging his paddle into the current with renewed vigor. "We've had enough trouble with live warriors without havin' to deal with the spirit kind!"

The travelers continued their journey for several more days until they came to a stockade overlooking the Juniata from a sharp bluff. Jack nodded with approval when he saw that the fort commanded a deep ravine leading down to the river. He also noted that the forest had been cut back from Fort Granville's other three sides to improve its defensive capabilities.

"Lookee there!" shrilled Hawkins. "Ain't that a grand sight up yonder?"

"Hope we're in time for supper," said Will.

"Me, too!" cracked Bob. "I'm hungry enough to eat skunk guts."

After beaching their canoe, Jack, Will, and Bob trudged up the steep incline to Fort Granville. They progressed unchallenged until they arrived at the gate. Finally, a scraggly militiaman dressed in unkempt clothes stepped from the shadows to ask meekly, "What's your business here, friends?"

"We's come to collect fer these fine Delaware scalps," hollered Winslow loud enough for the whole encampment to hear.

"S-S-Scalps?" stuttered the sentry.

"From a raiding party we chased off," added Cutler. "They burned out some folks up the West Branch of the Susquehanna."

"What else is new?" mumbled the guard. "I best take you to Captain Ward."

The woodsmen followed their guide into the fort compound where rows of tents were set up next to a rude cabin that served as the headquarters and supply house. When they entered the building, a forlorn officer wearing a brown day coat looked up from his desk. He was scribbling a hasty letter with a quill pen, and he cleared his throat before inquiring, "Who are these men, Corporal Turner?"

"Wall now, I'm Bearbite Bob Winslow," bawled the old trapper, "an' I brung ya the scalps o' three murderin' Delaware. That's three hundred ninety pieces o' eight ya owes me."

"Three hundred ninety dollars?" snorted the captain. "How am I supposed to pay you that when I barely have three rounds of ammunition per man? I've sent countless letters to Governor Morris pleading for powder and provisions, only to have three popinjays stride into my office thinking I'm the treasurer of Pennsylvania."

"But we're here to help," replied Will crossly. "And we have full horns of powder and plenty of round balls."

"We want to sign up fer the rangers, too," added Hawkins. "I know every inch o' this here wilderness an' have been to Kit-Han-Ne."

Captain Ward's face brightened with the woodmen's words, and, after looking them up and down, he thundered, "Then, welcome, gentlemen. We sure can use more long rifles, and. . .you have ammunition, you say? Corporal Turner, take these soldiers outside and assign them a tent. We ran out of beans this morning, but I'm sure there's still a little fatback we can feed them."

CHAPTER NINETEEN: FORT GRANVILLE

A week after they arrived, Jack and his friends learned for themselves how desperate things were at Fort Granville. They were on guard duty that summer morning when a large Delaware war party appeared suddenly outside the gate. Waiting impatiently for the command to fire, they watched the hideously painted braves dance, howl and gyrate for over an hour.

As Bearbite and Lightnin' exchanged angry glances, Captain Jacobs marched boldly forward to yelp, "You inside! We challenge you come out and fight! Or do you cower like dogs at sight of us?"

"We cower to no one!" rumbled Captain Ward. "Leave, or we'll shoot you like dogs!"

Ward's answer drove the Indians into a more intense frenzy. Brandishing tomahawks and muskets, they hurled insults against the stockade walls until Hawkins wondered why they didn't drive them off with gunfire. Finally, with a prolonged whoop, the Lenni Lenape divided into smaller bands around noon and disappeared into the gloom of the forest.

"Shouldn't we send out scouts to see what them varmints is up to?" asked Jack after all had become quiet again.

"C-C-Can't risk the men," stammered Corporal Turner with fear stamped on his sallow cheeks.

"Or the ammunition," added another soldier.

"Or the food they'd carry," croaked a third man.

"Why are you so ill-provisioned?" asked Will.

"It's the Quakers in control of the provincial council who won't give us what we need," growled an irate officer. "It's because their religion is against war. The damn savages will have to burn Philadelphia before they act!"

"Aye, Lieutenant Armstrong, that'd get 'em quakin' in their boots," guffawed a rawboned private.

"That's all that will," grumbled the lieutenant. "In March a wagonload of corpses killed by the Indians was driven back and forth in front of a Friends' Meeting House. Even that did nothing to sway the Quaker elders to improve frontier defenses."

Later that morning, a panicked group of settlers tore up the road to the fort. There were five somber men, two scared women, and ten blubbering children. They drove before them a milk cow and a herd of lowing cattle. A wounded farmer hobbled along behind, and he pleaded as they approached the gate, "Let us in. Please! Indians shot me. I need patched up."

"We haven't enough medicine to treat our own men," shouted Lieutenant Armstrong from atop the wall, "but we'll do what we can for you."

For the next two weeks runners brought news of the havoc caused by Captain Jacobs' war parties. After it was learned that a nearby family had been burned out and captured, Bearbite muttered to Jack and Will, "We didn't join this army to rot in no fort. Let's go sniff around on our own."

"Not without orders you won't!" exclaimed Captain Ward, overhearing Bob's whispers. "We expect discipline from our men."

The next morning a request came from Tuscarora Valley for troops to protect the farmers while they harvested grain. Captain Ward assembled his force in the fort compound and selected only his best men for the expedition. Turning to Lieutenant Armstrong, he said, "I leave you in command here. We haven't seen any sign of the Delaware since that arrogant Jacobs' challenge, so you should have nothing to worry about."

"Hey, ain't ya takin' us?" griped Winslow as the captain marched his men out the gate. "We's the best scouts this side o' the Allegheny."

"Then, tonight you'll enjoy scouting the inside of your tent until you learn to follow orders," snapped Ward. "In the meantime, you and your fellow rangers can climb yonder wall to look for Indians."

The captain's force had no sooner disappeared down the trail to the south when Bearbite, Jack, and Will saw shadows skulking in the distance forest. Soon, it became apparent that the Delaware had reunited and were supported by a white-coated company of French regulars. As Chief Jacobs and a slender officer stood just out of rifle range to jabber and gesture toward the stockade, Will asked, "Isn't that the same gent who led the French at Fort Necessity?"

"The same devil, ya mean!" spat Bearbite.

"That's Captain Villiers," confirmed Hawkins. "He was stirrin' up trouble at Kit-Han-Ne while I was there, too."

Suddenly, a mighty whoop rose from the Indians, and they unleashed a volley of musket balls that showered off the stout walls of Fort Granville. "Keep your heads down," ordered Lieutenant Armstrong. "Unless they got cannons, they can't do us a bit of harm."

The French and Indians fired five more ineffectual rounds until musket smoke obscured the field between the fort and the woods. Using the smoke for cover, the Delaware crept closer to shoot at the stronghold. Disobeying the order to stay down, Bearbite drilled one of the advancing braves through the chest, while Will and Jack killed two others. They ducked behind the wall to reload and then bounced back up to blast three Frenchmen. Their fire was so deadly that the rest of the attacking force withdrew to the safety of the trees.

Sporadic gunfire echoed from the forest until nightfall. When it grew eerily still, Bob said, "Them varmints couldn'ta give up. They outnumber us three to one."

"They's out there all right," grunted Hawkins, "an' ya kin bet yer topknot they ain't playin' black fish."

Jack, Will, and Bearbite didn't wait long before they heard whispers of movement coming up the ravine from the river. These progressed to within fifteen feet of the fort before the woodsmen split the night with three tongues of fire from their long rifles. Yelps of pain echoed from below, followed by a lone answering musket shot.

Before Hawkins and his friends could reload, renewed scurrying was followed by struck sparks and the glow of blazing pine knots. Animated warriors then popped from the gloom and hurled burning missiles against the fort. Even a second barrage from the rangers' rifles did little to deter the determined braves. They continued to bombard the palisade until the logs burst into bright flames.

When the night was alive with fire, wave after wave of howling fiends rushed to renew the assault. The conflagration aided the attackers' aim, and their bullets whined like bees past Hawkins' head. Smoke billowed from the burning wall to choke him, too, until Jack clambered from the catwalk, followed by his wheezing mates.

(Photo courtesy of Randy Quinn)

With no one to hinder them, the French and Delaware swarmed to the very walls of Fort Granville. Expectantly, the insurgents waited as flames licked up the stockade. When a large hole burned through the logs, the Indians raised a hellish commotion. Then, they surged forward to shoot through the gap with telling effect. Their first volley felled two gawking settlers, while subsequent shots killed a retreating private and wounded another in the knee.

Finally, Lieutenant Armstrong led a squad of defenders toward the breach in his defense. As the men swung into position, a Frenchman yelled from outside, "You haven't a chance, monsieurs. Why not surrender?"

"Oui, let me talk to them," Jack heard a white-faced private beg. "I am part French and can bargain in their own language."

"The first word of French you speak in this engagement," snarled Armstrong, "and I'll blow your brains out. Come on, we can put out this fire!"

"How we gonna do that?" cried another cringing soldier. "We run outta water two days ago."

"You can man a shovel, can't you?" snapped the lieutenant. "Get to it!"

While Armstrong and his firefighters madly dug and flung dirt at the ever-widening hole in the front wall, Hawkins led his friends behind the tents at the rear of the compound. "My bacon is really fried if Captain Jacobs takes this fort," he croaked. "He'll gut an' skin me quicker 'n them cattle."

"We're in a tight spot, all right," murmured Will. "We can't surrender. That's for sure."

"Wall now, if them savages kin burn theirselves inta the fort, why can't we burn our way out?" chortled Bob, pulling a flaming log out of a campfire. "You boys set the back wall ablaze, an' I'll hold them devils off 'til we kin git."

Using the tents to hide their efforts, Jack and Will followed Winslow's biding. Bearbite, meanwhile, knelt to shoot any hostile who attacked them. It was then that he saw Lieutenant Armstrong struck down by a round ball through the heart.

After Armstrong crumbled to the ground, the din inside the fort became deafening. The shrill shrieks of the Indians mingled with bellowing cows, wails of children, and the screams of hysterical women. Finally, a commanding voice barked through the flaming gap in the wall, "I am Chevalier Louis Coulon de Villiers. As an officer and gentleman, I guarantee you'll be spared if you surrender now."

Villiers' words led Bearbite to where the officer stood wreathed in smoke, and the scout fired a desperate shot at him. After missing the shadowy Frenchman by inches, Bob yelled, "Don't listen to 'im, er we're all gone beavers!"

Ignoring Winslow's warning, Corporal Turner dropped his musket and sprinted toward the fort gates. Bob rammed another ball in his barrel and drew down on the streaking coward. Before he could squeeze the trigger, Turner swung open the doors with a yawning grate. A howling mob of savages swarmed through the opening, and the stunned colonials became prisoners.

Bob muttered a string of disgusted curses. Then, he watched the private who'd been shot through the knee stagger painfully from the shadows. Using his gun as a crutch, the limping soldier approached Chevalier Villiers as he strode triumphantly into the compound accompanied by Captain Jacobs. "Monsieur," cried the wounded man, "I am so glad you saved me. I am Brandon, a Catholic, and want to join your brave army."

Villiers was about to shake Brandon's hand when Captain Jacobs saw that the man could not walk. Jerking a tomahawk from his belt, he split the traitor's skull with one powerful clout and then howled, "My Delaware braves, victory is ours! Take their muskets! Take their powder! And gather up the captives!"

"But what about Lieutenant Armstrong?" Bearbite heard a quaking private ask. "Won't you let us bury him?"

"Mais non!" grunted the suddenly callous Villiers. "Did the skulking dog, George Washington, not murder my brother? Why should I then so honor this man?"

"But he's an officer like yerself," reminded the private. "It'd only take a minute ta bury Edward in that pit we dug to throw dirt on the fire."

"You heard Villiers!" shouted Captain Jacobs, baring his knife. "Let him rot!"

As the prisoners gasped in disbelief, Jacobs bent over the fallen Armstrong and yanked the scalp from his head. Waving the bloody hair in his hand, the chief boasted, "I can take any fort that will catch fire! I will make peace with the English when they teach me to make gun powder!"

(Photo courtesy of Randy Quinn)

Just then, Will hissed to Bearbite, "Our fire's burned through. Let's go!"

Winslow shifted the sights of his long rifle until they rested on Captain Jacobs' sneering smile. As Bob touched off a perfect shot, a celebrating warrior danced in front of the chief to have his brains blown out the side of his head. Jacobs' grin turned to a surprised scowl as gore splattered across his face. "Get that assassin!" he finally bellowed. "Now!"

Bob sprang to his feet, and in three bounds, burst out the back door his friends had burned through the palisade. In an instant, two hatchet-waving pursuers surged through the opening only to be blown backward by Will and Jack. The woodsmen then turned and ran until the night swallowed them up.

"Where do we go from here?" panted Cutler when the burning stockade was but a glimmer on the horizon.

"Better find us another fort," whispered Hawkins, "'cause this whole valley's swarmin' with hostiles."

CHAPTER TWENTY: THE DEVIL TO PAY

Jack, Will, and Bob spent several days hiding in the dense woods. They kept a sharp lookout for Delaware war parties while surviving on spring water, arrowleaf roots, and berries. Finally, Hawkins murmured, "I reckon it's safe to head upriver fer Fort Shirley now. Once them braves got to plunderin' Granville, they musta fergot all 'bout us."

"Don't fergit the murderin' they done, neither," grunted Bearbite. "That shoulda satisfied their bloodlust at least fer the time bein'. After watchin' the pleasure Captain Jacobs took in rippin' off that lieutenant's hair, I reckon my scalp huntin' days is over."

"So it's back to beaver trapping and squawin', is it?" needled Will.

"That's right! A woodsman's gotta do what he does best."

"'Specially, when he don't know the treasurer of Pennsylvania from a fort captain," snickered Jack, slipping off into the forest before Bearbite could refute him.

With Hawkins in the lead, the woodsmen crept to the banks of the Juniata River and checked both directions for Indian canoes before sneaking upstream. Often, they waded through the shallows to hide their tracks before again stealing along the rocks on the shoreline. Any rattling branch made them freeze. Any crow caw caused them to raise their rifles.

After a week of cautious travel, Jack peered out of a hemlock thicket and saw an army encampment swarming with activity just ahead. Before he could step out of the brush, a stern voice demanded, "Who's there?"

Jack looked up again to find himself staring down the wrong end of three musket barrels. The guns were held by professional soldiers dressed in green coats faced in red. By the glint in these sentries' eyes, Hawkins figured they were itching to use their weapons.

"I'm Lightnin' Hawkins," replied the woodsman with a disarming smile. "My friends here are Bearbite Bob an' Big Cat Cutler. We's come to join yer rangers."

"Look who have here," barked a familiar voice from behind the sentries. "And just how did you happen to escape when my whole garrison at Fort Granville got killed or captured?"

The guards snapped to attention as Captain Ward, accompanied by a robust colonel, came striding toward them. "Well, Hawkins?" asked Ward impatiently.

"By keepin' our heads, not like them other damn fools. The only fella who showed any grit was Lieutenant Armstrong, an' he got scalped by Captain Jacobs fer his efforts."

"Then, there'll be the devil to pay!" growled the other officer in a thick Irish brogue. "That's me brother the heathen butchered!"

"I'm so sorry, Colonel Armstrong," sighed Ward. "If I hadn't been called out to guard those farmers, none of this would have happened."

"Aye, but at least Governor Morris authorized our expedition after your men's sacrifice at Granville. Hawkins' news makes it personal!"

Colonel John Armstrong's sudden display of anger caused Jack to study him more closely. The colonel's tricorn was jammed down over a thick crop of reddish brown hair. His steely eyes squinted with purpose and were accented by crow's-feet that crinkled on his ruddy, thirty-eight year old face. The silver gorget, denoting his rank, hung around a bull neck. His bulky officer's coat could not hide his muscularity.

"But colonel, sir," croaked Hawkins with a clumsy salute, "how will ya exact yer revenge?"

"By a burnin' Kit-Han-Ne to the ground!"

"An' I'm the man ta lead ya there, bein' I escaped from Captain Jacobs' own house."

"Then, maybe ye can tell me if John Baker's map be accurate," replied Armstrong, producing a folded piece of paper from his cartridge box.

"Right as rain!" exclaimed Jack after studying the map for a moment. "How did Baker come by it?"

"He drew it from memory after slippin' from the devils' hands in March. He be comin' along on me expedition to settle a score of his own."

"Count us in, too," enthused Will Cutler. "We're all veterans of Braddock's fight."

"Then, ye be welcome," replied the colonel.

"But they're not disciplined," objected Captain Ward. "They wanted to go find the Indians on their own."

"So we'll use them as scouts, we will. They'll make perfect rangers. Go inside the fort, men, an' get ye a hot meal."

"Thank you, sir," answered Will. "We won't let you down."

When the officers returned to checking the perimeter of their camp, Jack and his friends meandered into Fort Shirley to find the cook tent.

After they entered, a jovial Irishman with a thick red beard said, "All the new dogs come sniffin' around here. Have a plate of me stew, boys, an' set yerselves down fer a while."

"Ya call this stew?" joshed Bearbite. "It smells more like a week-old deer carcass."

"Aye, and an old buzzard like you should be more 'n happy to gobble it up," chortled the cook.

"I'm jess as good at flyin' as I am eatin'," cackled Winslow, pulling three scalps from his possibles bag. "Why, jess last month I swooped down an' snatched the hair from these Delaware. Any chance I kin trade them scalps fer powder an' provisions?"

"As much as ye boys can carry," winked the cook. "I happen to be the quartermaster, too."

The next morning at first light, Lieutenant Colonel Armstrong assembled his seven companies on the parade ground outside Fort Shirley. It was cool for late August, and after pacing back and forth on the dewy grass, he stopped to scan the three hundred faces he would lead against Kit-Han-Ne. There were green-coated regulars of the Pennsylvania Second Battalion, militia companies dressed in smocks and leggings, and buckskin-clad trappers and traders. Regardless of the degree of his military experience, each man bore an air of resolve that brought an appreciative smile to the colonel's lips.

Colonel Armstrong was also happy to have a well-respected captain in charge of each company. After noting the sincere demeanor of John Potter, Hance Hamilton, Dr. Hugh Mercer, Edward Ward, Joseph Armstrong, and Reverend John Steel, he knew these officers would not fail him no matter how hot the action got.

Finally, Armstrong threw back his shoulders, clicked his heels, and ordered his men to attention in a deep, booming voice. Afterward, he blared, "Captain Potter, step forward and report. How many men do ye have in rank this fine day?"

"Forty-seven brave Scotch Irish from Cumberland Valley," chimed the officer. "All present and accounted for, sir!"

Potter's reply brought a rousing cheer from his men. After their huzzahs echoed off into the forest, Armstrong received equal enthusiasm from the other six companies in turn. When roll call was complete, the colonel rumbled, "Today, we embark on an important mission. Each one here has had friends, relatives, and neighbors butchered by the bloody denizens of Kit-Han-Ne. It's time to take the war to them, lads! Fire for fire! Blood for blood!"

Again, the parade ground shook with a thunderous hooray. Then, the drummers struck up a marching cadence that set the army's feet in motion. Fort Shirley had barely faded from view, however, when the drumming came to an abrupt halt. This was due to the roughness of the road that caused the men to break rank and stream in single file past mud holes and around windfalls blocking the trail.

"I'm glad them stinkin' drummers stopped their racket," grunted Bearbite when they tramped along in silence.

"Er every brave from here to the Allegheny would know we was comin'," asserted Jack.

"We sure don't need that," agreed Will. "Much less the headache I was getting."

"Jess think how yer head would be throbbin' with a hatchet stuck in it," muttered Bob.

(Photo courtesy of Randy Quinn)

The march continued for three days under a sweltering sun. Sweat soaked the men's uniforms and stung their eyes as they tramped along. Wearily, they put one foot in front of the other when they weren't slipping in mud or evading briars that overran the road. Even the militia was too tired to grumble by the time Armstrong's army reached the beaver dams near Franks Town where an advanced party waited for them.

The colonel ordered his men to set up camp in a shady glen. With a collective sigh, they stumbled out of rank to stack their rifles and tend the mud-splattered pack horses. Soon, the air was heavy with the thud of hatchets as tent pegs were pounded into the baked summer earth. The digging of fire pits followed by the crackling of lit tinder signaled the beginning of a long-awaited supper.

While his soldiers prepared beans and bacon, Armstrong sought out Hawkins and said, "It's time ye and your friends join our scouts. Tomorrow, we'll be walking the Kittanning Indian Trail, and I'll need ye to keep us from an ambush."

"Yes, sir!" exclaimed Jack. "Scoutin's what we do best!"

The army was underway again by mid-morning with Lightnin', Will, Bob, and the other pathfinders fanned out a mile ahead of the main party. The woodsmen were once more in their element and exchanged grins as they scanned the brush for signs of the enemy. Their smiles quickly faded when they skated down a dip into a nasty morass filled with water and black muck. There, they slogged along for several miles through knee-deep mud that taxed every joint and muscle in their legs. Swarms of blood-thirsty mosquitoes added to their discomfort until they splashed ashore at the foot of a broken hill.

The trail then wound up a steep slope slippery with loose gravel and rocks. The scouts' wet moccasins made the going even slicker, and they repeatedly fell on their faces after every few steps they managed. Finally, they were forced to walk sideways like clumsy ducks to scale the treacherous hillside.

Just as Winslow reached the summit, he winced in pain and grabbed for his shin. Collapsing in a heap, he cussed and gritted his teeth until a nearby scout knelt to assist him. Pulling spare leggings from his possibles bag, the ranger wound them tightly around Bob's left leg until the tension faded from the old hunter's face.

"Thanks," panted Winslow. "I reckon I kin make it now."

"No problem," replied the other scout. "You must be harder 'n flint ta have tramped as far as ya did, grandpa."

"That's 'Bearbite' to you," growled Bob, shooting the fellow a withering glare. "Armstrong wouldn't have made me a ranger if I be a blunderin' old fool."

"Sorry, Bearbite. I didn't mean no harm. Let me help ya to yer feet, so we don't fall behind the rest of the boys."

"I kin get up myself! Why, if this be the worst ill I git from this raid, I'll be out wrestlin' she-bears come Saturday."

"Er at least a Delaware squaw," chuckled the other pathfinder with an amused shake of his head.

CHAPTER TWENTY-ONE: ATTACK ON KIT-HAN-NE

When Colonel Armstrong had marched his army to within fifty miles of Kit-Han-Ne, he commanded the soldiers to fall out and rest their fatigued legs. After he got his men bivouacked, he sent for Jack Hawkins, Thomas Burke, and James Chalmers. Looking the scouts square in the eye, Armstrong instructed, "I want ye to check the path ahead, so we're not surprised by savages. I chose you because you've all been to the Delaware village."

"That's right," chortled Burke. "Me an' James skinned more 'n one Injun in our dealin's there."

"Then, ye won't mind creeping to Kit-Han-Ne to reconnoiter the place for me?"

"Not at all, sir," replied Jack. "I know every house an' who lives in it."

Hawkins and the two old traders left camp in a dense mist that made them nearly invisible as they slipped northwest up the rough trail. Ghost-like, they flitted along for several hours until Hawkins whispered to Chalmers, "Wall now, there's the fork in the trail where I done tricked Captain Jacobs an' made my getaway. We can't be more 'n a couple mile from the village."

"Then, the whole trail must be free of Injuns if we ain't run into none yet," croaked James, wiping cold sweat from his forehead. "Let's head back."

"But the colonel wanted us to spy on Kit-Han-Ne," protested Jack.

"No use in this fog," grunted Thomas. "It's time ta leave."

Reluctantly, Hawkins turned and followed the other scouts. They tramped wearily all night to return to their camp. When they ducked to enter John Armstrong's tent to file their report, the sun was just peeping over the horizon.

"The path's completely clear," said Chalmers after giving a tired salute.

"But what about the village?" demanded the colonel. "How many Delaware are there? Did you spot any French?"

"It were too foggy ta see much," answered Burke evasively, spraying the ground with tobacco juice. "Ain't that right, Hawkins?"

"It's like he said, sir," muttered Jack.

"Then, ye couldn't have looked too hard," growled John Armstrong. "You men go rest. I'll send out fresh scouts when we get underway. They'll be younger fellows with sharper eyes."

And get underway Armstrong did, leading his army on a double-time forced march that cut the distance to Kit-Han-Ne to twenty miles. As they trotted along, Winslow's limp grew more pronounced until Will locked arms with him to keep him moving. Mercifully, when Bob's pain became almost unbearable, a ranger returned from the advanced party to hiss, "Colonel, we jess spotted three er four hostiles camped around a fire up yonder. It'd be no problem capturin' the rascals. What do ya want us to do?"

It was now dark, and John Armstrong glanced warily into the shadows around him before saying, "It's too risky to attack the heathen in this murk. What if one should sneak away and warn the village? Lieutenant Hogg, take twelve men and watch them 'til sunup. After ye hear our firing, cut the devils down."

"Yes, sir!" replied the lieutenant. "We'll give 'em hell!"

After Hogg's detail slipped off into the gloom, Armstrong ordered two men to stay with the pack horses. Then, he led his army into the dense brush to circle around the camped Indians ahead. It was ankle-twisting work scrambling across slippery boulders and over fallen timber. Luckily, the moon rose to bathe the forest in a steady glow that allowed the colonials to complete their detour and return to the trail.

(Photo courtesy of Greg Rearick)

After what seemed like forever to the hobbling Winslow, Armstrong's force reached the Allegheny River. Here, the colonel called Baker and Hawkins to his side and whispered, "Does any of this look familiar to you boys?"

Before either could answer, the beating of war dance drums reverberated though the woods toward them. Using the sound as a guide,

Armstrong again led his troops forward through the moonlight. They had just crept to within sight of Kit-Han-Ne when a singular whistle split the night, causing the officer to duck into the brush.

"Did they spot us?" gasped Armstrong to John Baker, who knelt next to him.

"No, that was a brave whistlin' fer his squaw," chuckled Baker. "Must have ro-mance on his mind."

Armstrong rose in time to watch the Indian build a fire just below him in the cornfield between the river and the town. The brave then cleaned his rifle and fired it before snuggling with the girl who ran to meet him. Soon, fires sprang up from all corners of the field. When Baker saw his colonel's quizzical frown, he explained, "The heat has brung the Injuns outdoors to sleep. Them smoky fires is to drive away gnats."

After the moon set and things became quiet in Kit-Han-Ne, Armstrong motioned for Captain Steel's company to sneak along the hill and position themselves at the upper part of the town farthest from the river. For twenty heart-pounding minutes Jack, Will, and Bob crouched behind the colonel until he leaped up to howl, "Every man do for himself!"

In the next instant, the colonials spilled into the cornfield yelling and firing their weapons. Jack saw a Delaware scramble to his feet, and instead of shooting him, clubbed the brave to the ground with his rifle butt. Red Hawk's face had flooded into Hawkins' memory, and he suddenly didn't want to shoot anyone. He loped along in a trance remembering the laughter he shared with his little brother, while Bearbite and Will filled the dawn with rifle blasts and wild whoops.

(Photo courtesy of Randy Quinn)

It was fully light when the soldiers entered Kit-Han-Ne, and Jack and his friends surrounded the first house they encountered. A surprised warrior stepped outside and found three guns pointed at him. "White men!" he screeched, and soon after Hawkins heard Captain Jacobs' war whoop reverberate from the center of town.

"You men," shouted Colonel Armstrong, "secure that prisoner and come on!"

As Will and Jack tied up the captured brave, Hawkins was relieved to see a steady stream of Delaware women and children running for the shelter of the forest. "I sure hope Willow and Red Hawk git away," he jabbered, searching vainly for a glimpse of them.

"Me, too!" yelled Will. "I can't believe there's a bounty on women and boys."

"Fergit them," yelped Winslow. "Look! Our colonel's got his hands full!"

(Photo courtesy of Greg Rearick)

Glancing down the hill, Jack saw Armstrong's company had surrounded Captain Jacobs' house. The chief and his family were shooting through loopholes in the log walls, and their accurate fire knocked one green-coated soldier after another to the ground.

"Let's go!" exhorted Will. "They sure need us marksmen."

With Bearbite hobbling after them, Cutler and Hawkins sprinted off to join the assault below. They had just reached John Armstrong's side when a fresh Indian volley ripped through the ranks. Hawkins heard the whoosh of bullets sing past his ear and then watched in horror as Will and the colonel collapsed in a spray of blood.

Bending low, Hawkins scrambled to attend his fallen comrades. First, he crouched over Will to examine the gore oozing from a nasty wound in the lad's side. Ripping open Cutler's shirt, he tried desperately to staunch the flow of blood with a folded handkerchief.

As Will lapsed into unconsciousness, Hawkins heard Colonel Armstrong groan for him. With Jack's help, the groggy officer rose holding his bloody shoulder. Staggering back into rank, he yipped, "Come on, men. Keep shooting!"

The colonials now were receiving fire from many stout dwellings where the Indians had barricaded themselves. Thus protected, the braves shot the soldiers at will, while bullets ricocheted harmlessly off the thick, log walls of their cabins. Alarmed at the number of casualties falling around him, Armstrong finally challenged, "Is there none of you lads who will set fire to these rascals that wounded me and killed so many of our men?"

An angry growl rose from the ranks and several colonials dropped their rifles, dug flint and steel from their haversacks, and struck sparks into a hurriedly gathered pile of rubbish. When the trash burst into flames, soldiers lit sticks and rushed off to ignite the dwellings around them. They succeeded in setting every house ablaze except the Jacobs' place where accurate shooting still kept them at bay.

Finally, after a private and a sergeant were gunned down by the taunting Captain Jacobs, Bearbite grabbed a burning brand, flourished it over his head, and shambled toward the fortress. Dust kicked up around his legs from shots that missed him by inches, causing Winslow to weave and bob with a more pronounced limp. After another round blew the slouch hat from his head, he screeched like a cougar and rumbled toward the cabin door. He was only a few steps away when a single blast rang out. The old trapper yelped once and then toppled forward, extinguishing the torch under his body. As

Bearbite gasped and gurgled, Jack heard Young Jacobs' unmistakable victory whoop knife through a loophole in the wall.

A mighty groan passed through the colonial ranks before a lean, quick-footed soldier named John Ferguson ripped a piece of burning bark from a neighboring house and streaked for the Jacobs' stronghold. Miraculously, he evaded the bullets that sang past his flailing legs. Reaching a side wall, he held the bark against it until it caught fire. With smoke swelling around him, Ferguson raced again for his own lines. Spurred on by the cheers of his comrades, he somehow returned unscathed.

As flames licked from the Indian dwellings and the smoke thickened, Jack cringed when a warrior's strong voice echoed from a nearby hut. He knew the brave was singing his death song to show his scorn for his enemies. Then, from another house, Hawkins heard a wailing squaw scolded to silence by her husband. In the next instant, the couple bolted from the blazing doorway toward the cornfield only to be struck down by a volley of round balls. The blood-drunk soldiers feverishly reloaded and drew down on a string of white captives who burst from the same dwelling. Only Lightnin's yell of "Friends! Don't shoot!" saved the lives of those who dashed to their freedom.

Captain Jacobs' house was burning briskly now, too, and Colonel Armstrong shouted to those trapped inside, "Your town is on fire, you dogs, you! Come out and surrender!"

"I'm a man!" exclaimed the enraged voice of the chief. "I'll not be prisoner!"

"Then, you'll burn!" snarled the colonel.

"I _eat_ fire!" yelped Captain Jacobs in reply.

The building blazed for several more minutes before choking Indians burst from the front door. Jack gaped wide-eyed as a hail of bullets cut down Young Jacobs, Willow, and three of their cousins. Just then, Red Hawk staggered coughing from the hut, and a sneering corporal raised his musket to blast the boy. Before he could shoot, Hawkins rushed the soldier and knocked the gun from his hands. In a blur of motion, Jack whirled and streaked to tackle his little brother. They hit the ground as another salvo of musket balls whined over their heads.

(Photo courtesy of Randy Quinn)

"Hold yer fire!" screeched Hawkins, covering the boy with his body. "He ain't harmed no one!"

"You ain't foolin' me," growled the angry corporal. "You jess want him fer a prisoner."

"That's right!" snapped Thomas Burke. "Alive, that whelp will fetch ya a hundred thirty dollars. His scalp's only worth fifty."

"Do ya think I'd sell my own brother?" bleated Jack. "What kind o' fiends have you become?"

The soldiers' answer was drowned out by another loud volley, and Hawkins looked up to see Captain Jacobs tumble through a loft window. Before the chief landed, his burly torso was rent by so many bullets that he couldn't even cry out in defiance.

As Colonel Armstrong strode to inspect the riddled body, a sergeant had already ripped off the chief's scalp. "Aye, it's Jacobs all right," cried the excited soldier. "No other Injun wore his hair like that!"

"An' look at the rascal's new powder horn an' pouch, colonel," babbled a militiaman. "I heard he traded yer brother's boots fer 'em after he burned Fort Granville."

"Hey, the chief's woman is over here," cackled James Chalmers. "She give me a beaver plew fer that ornament she's wearin' in her hair."

Red Hawk squirmed out from under Jack and rushed weeping to his mother's side. Two soldiers pushed him roughly away, hacked off the woman's scalp, and waved it jubilantly in the air. Numbly, Jack watched their brutality as Willow's acts of kindness replayed in his brain. He was unaware of the tears streaming from his eyes until his little brother came running to embrace him.

CHAPTER TWENTY-TWO: THE RETREAT

"An' look who we's got here," gloated James Chalmers. "It's the chief's son!"

Red Hawk glanced in fear at the old trader. Then, he buried his face in Jack's chest. After shifting the boy behind him, Hawkins raised his long rifle to keep the other white man at bay.

Instead of harassing Red Hawk, Chalmers scrambled to Young Jacobs' corpse and gasped, "Why, this varmint must be seven feet long. We should git a double bounty fer the likes o' him."

"But what's ya gonna use fer proof when he ain't got a scalp lock on that shaved skull o' his?" asked a nearby militiaman.

"I'll jess have to cut off his head!"

Hawkins looked sharply away as Chalmers yanked a hatchet from his belt and severed the dead giant's neck with four precise blows. Jack should have been elated by the demise of his tormentor. Instead, he only felt sorrow that poured in from all five senses until Kit-Han-Ne became a nightmarish blur. Young Jacobs' decapitated head, the stench of singed bark and flesh, the howling of battle-mad soldiers, the pasty taste of fear, and the cold touch of his unfired rifle made the ground whirl and the sky fade to nothing.

The blaring of Colonel Armstrong's voice suddenly cut through the darkness, and Jack returned to himself. "Don't you hear that gunfire across the river?" Armstrong shouted. "Though it took 'em all morning, Shingas' braves are rallying.

Time to round up the prisoners, collect the wounded, and get the hell out of here!"

"But we haven't destroyed the cornfield," reminded Ward.

"No, but we torched every house. Let's get moving."

"What about the dead?" asked Jack.

"Bring them, too, or the savages will mutilate their bodies."

"An' hurry!" pleaded a freed white captive. "I heard two bateaux o' Frenchies is comin' today to join the Delaware an' attack Fort Shirley."

Lightnin' and Red Hawk rushed to where Bob Winslow lay sprawled out before the Jacobs' cabin. He was still breathing, so they dragged him a safe distance from the licking flames. They had just reached the ruins of the smoldering council house when the stored gunpowder inside the boy's home ignited in a deafening explosion.

(Photo courtesy of Greg Rearick)

Reeling from the concussion, Jack and his brother watched in amazement as the roof flew into kindling. In the next instant, a small child and the leg of an Indian were blown so high in the air that they appeared as nothing before falling into the distant cornfield. After the victims plummeted to the ground, Red Hawk lapsed into mournful silence. Finally, he croaked, "Poor Sunfish. A-A-And his son. T-T-That could have been me. . ."

Red Hawk blinked back his tears when he heard Bearbite moan feebly. Then, he and Jack bent to make the old woodsman more comfortable. "Looks like I'm a gone beaver," whispered Bob. "What I need is a shot o' rum, but I know ya ain't got none. I-I-I wants ya to have my rifle an' kit, Lightnin'. Say goodbye to Will fer me. Say. . ."

Winslow's voice trailed off into a vague rattle. After the light faded from his pale, blue eyes, Hawkins closed Bearbite's eyelids. Squeezing his friend's dead hand, Jack mumbled, "I'm gonna miss ya, ya old coot. We was in some mighty tight scrapes together, an' ya always got us through. See ya ag'in up yonder where there's endless beaver an' the huntin' ain't never poor."

After gunpowder exploded in another nearby house, Lightnin' bounced nervously to his feet. "Carry this brave man from the field," he yelled to a retreating militia company that ran toward them. "You seen him give his life fer the rest o' us."

While the soldiers snatched up Bearbite's body and hurried off with it, Jack and Red Hawk scrambled to find the wounded Cutler. They searched feverishly as more doomed huts blew up in every corner of the flaming village. Finally, they saw Will lying ghastly pale exactly where Jack had left him.

With Red Hawk's help, Hawkins hoisted the groaning Cutler onto his back and staggered into the cornfield toward the Allegheny River. The boy hustled along at his side carrying Bob's long rifle, powder horn, and possibles bag.

"Why we not follow other soldiers?" asked Red Hawk when he saw that Colonel Armstrong's men were retreating up the hills behind Kit-Han-Ne to the south.

"They ain't any different 'n yer braves," grunted Jack. "They scalp an' kill an' destroy anyone they think is an enemy--even yer ma an' helpless children."

"Then, where we go?"

"Upriver to Ishua Town."

"But you never get by Shingas' braves."

"I will if I look like one of 'em."

Hawkins laid his wounded friend gently on the ground near a dead Delaware warrior. Rummaging through the slain man's pouch, he produced a clay pot of war paint and dabbed it all over his face. Next, Jack pulled out his knife and handed it to his brother. "Shave off my hair," he instructed. "Damn! I jess got it growed out the way I like it, an' now I'll be back to wearin' a scalp lock."

When Jack and Red Hawk tramped down the slope to the Allegheny, they were met by a howling war party incensed with anger and hate. The Delaware paid no attention to the disguised Hawkins even though he was carrying Cutler on his back. Instead, they shook their tomahawks, waved their muskets, and cursed every white man west of Philadelphia.

The woodsman walked boldly to one of the beached canoes the Indians had just guided from the west bank of the river and placed his unconscious friend in the middle of the craft. After Red Hawk got in the bow, Jack scrambled into the stern and pushed off. With strong, leisurely strokes, he dug his paddle into the current. As he steered upstream, he could hear a renewed round of musket shots from the warriors pushing into the cornfield.

Jack and Red Hawk had just gotten underway when Shingas and another brave came boiling downriver with two puny doe piled in their canoe between them. The chief and his companion were paddling for all they were worth directly toward Jack and Red Hawk. Hawkins' heart pounded with stabbing fear until Shingas cried, "So you caught one of the white dogs. Good! Take him to Custaloga Town where he never be found."

"Yes, uncle," said Red Hawk evenly. "We do just that."

"Why did I leave yesterday to hunt?" bemoaned the chief. "If I be here when white man come, their scalps would hang from every lodge pole."

"Hurry, uncle! Soldiers just now retreating."

"Then, I head them off. Cut them to pieces!"

Hawkins avoided eye contact with Shingas as the seething chief zoomed past. Jack continued to paddle with a slow, steady motion until he propelled his craft around a bend in the Allegheny. With the burning village finally out of sight, the woodsman issued a relieved whistle.

When Lightnin's heartbeat returned to normal, he whispered to Red Hawk, "Ya done good back there, little brother, not givin' us away to Shingas."

"That's because I want to be man like you, not him!"

"Why would ya say that?" asked Hawkins, blushing from the compliment.

"It because of what he made me do."

"Made ya do?"

"When war party bring back captives from Fort Granville, they sink stake in ground and tie up man who opened gates for them. Say him coward for betraying friends. Then, Shingas take man's scalp, and other braves stick red hot gun barrels and burning splinters into his body. Torture goes on for hours before Shingas pick me up, hand me hatchet, and order me to kill man. Had no choice but sink hatchet in his head."

"We all been asked ta do bad things in this here war," said Jack quietly. "An' it sure made ya grow up quick. That's why I want ya to keep Bearbite's rifle."

"You mean it?" murmured Red Hawk, casting a loving glance at the long rifle beside him.

"You're gonna need that gun when we goes trappin' together."

"Trapping?"

"Sure! There ain't no one I'd rather go in business with unless it be that golden-haired lad layin' there."

"But I know nothing of the white man's way of trapping."

"Well, ya learned the white man's game o' checkers quick enough," reminded Jack.

"Gronk! Gronk!" intoned Red Hawk with a reminiscent smile.

"An' I'll teach ya 'bout trappin' jess like I did Will."

Upon hearing his name, Cutler stirred and opened his eyes. Staring blankly at the sky, he cried, "Is that you calling me, Pa?"

"No, it's Lightnin'. You lie still, ya hear? We's goin' home where ya kin heal right proper."

"But I don't want to go back to England," fussed Cutler. "You can't make me, Pa!"

"Dip Will a cold drink from the river," Jack croaked to Red Hawk, tossing him a wooden cup he dug from his possibles bag. "He must be out o' his head with fever."

"I don't have the fever, Pa. I'm just burning with love for a beautiful Indian girl. Her name's Bright Star, and I love her, love her, Love Her, LOVE HER!"

"An' you'll be seein' her right quick, Will," assured Lightnin' in a soothing voice, "jess as soon as we pass though Delaware lands."

"Don't worry about them, Pa. We got all the Indians on the run. Pa! Pa! Look at them go!"

(Photo courtesy of Randy Quinn)

CHAPTER TWENTY-THREE: GIFTS

Jack and Red Hawk worked their canoe slowly upstream, stopping often to nurse Will. Instead of paddling until dusk, they made camp early the first evening to give Cutler a break from the jostling current. While they rested on the bank, crafts full of jabbering warriors streaked past them headed for the French forts near Lake Erie. From snatches of overheard conversation, Hawkins and his little brother learned that Kit-Han-Ne was deserted and in total ruin.

(Photo courtesy of Greg Rearick)

It took a month of loving care before Cutler was able to sit up for any length of time to enjoy the scenery along the Allegheny. Finally, one warm October afternoon they reached a familiar stretch of the river that caused Lightnin' to blurt,

"We's comin' up on Ishua Town, Will. You best lay yerself back down."

"But I'm much better," protested the lad, "after the coddling you and Red Hawk gave me."

"Hey, all we done is dress yer wound an' feed ya turtle soup 'til it come out yer ears."

"And don't forget that bearskin you got for me at Venango. I can't believe you risked stopping there, even if you are disguised as a Delaware. I sure thank you, though. I'd have died from the chills without it."

"Nothing too good for our partner," chimed Red Hawk. "You lay down like Swift Lightning say."

Reluctantly, Cutler curled up on the bottom of the canoe and covered himself with the bearskin. He had no sooner ducked out of sight when Hawkins shouted, "Wall, lookee there! Ain't that highlander a sight fer sore eyes!"

Jack pointed toward the riverbank just ahead, and Red Hawk turned to see a lanky white man fishing with a hand line. When the fellow noticed their canoe, he began dancing a merry jig and waving wildly. After they'd closed within shouting range, Red Hawk could hear him roaring in a thick Scottish brogue, "It's Lightnin' Jack Hawkins, it is! Welcome home, laddie! Welcome home!"

Hawkins steered the canoe directly for Alexander MacDonald and leaped ashore to shake hands with his friend. After they had exchanged hugs, as well, Mac asked, "And who be this ye have with you?"

"My Delaware brother, Red Hawk. If ya peer beneath that bearskin, you'll also see a close friend. After ya do, dash back to the village an' fetch Bright Star."

MacDonald's face blanched when he recognized Will Cutler lying prostrate on the floor of the canoe. "An' a where be B-B-Bearbite Bob?" he stammered after a telling silence.

"He died a hero. At Kit-Han-Ne. Will got badly wounded there, too."

Without waiting to hear any details, Mac whirled and streaked off in the direction of Ishua Town. A few minutes later he returned with two young women hard on his heels. The first threw herself at Hawkins and embraced him until it hurt. The other maiden stared curiously down at Will, emitted a little gasp, and buried her face in her hands.

"Ease up, girl," Hawkins begged Little Mink, "er you'll bust m' spine!" Then, he said to Bright Star, "Ain't ya gonna see what ails yer man? He's hurt mighty bad an' needs yer lovin' touch."

The princess glanced once more into the canoe and swallowed hard. Finally, she stepped hesitantly into the bobbing craft that Red Hawk steadied for her. Bending to her knees, she studied her husband's pale cheeks framed by an abundant shock of flaxen hair. It was the same face that she had found so handsome the year before, but the lips that had wooed her were now silent and blistered by fever.

Suddenly, Bright Star burst into tears and sobbed uncontrollably until Will's eyes fluttered open. When she saw a mixture of pain and love mirrored in his blue pupils, she cried to Alex, "H-H-Help me take husband back to longhouse. I nurse him. M-M-Make him well. . ."

Mac scrambled to do Bright Star's bidding, and together they hoisted Will to his feet. As they helped him limp gingerly onto the bank, the lad cried out in pain. Jack glanced toward Cutler with alarm. Then, he stifled a smirk when he saw Will's grimace was followed by a quick wink.

After his friends had shuffled past him up the path, Hawkins bent to kiss his wife long on the mouth. He could feel her heart beating as he held her tightly against him. He continued to embrace her until the darkness from the raid of Kit-Han-Ne had faded from his consciousness. Finally, he stepped back and said, "Darlin', I brung ya the gift I promised."

"Oh, show me! Show me!"

Grinning broadly, Jack turned and pointed toward Red Hawk. "Look. He's settin' right there."

In the next instant, the boy beached the canoe and ran to hug Little Mink. She kissed him tenderly on the forehead and purred, "Welcome to Ishua Town, my brother. You have grown since I last see you. How is your family?"

Red Hawk's muscles tensed, and he stared vacantly away. "I not remember," he mumbled.

"Not remember?" echoed Little Mink. "What you mean by that?"

"Now, don't go badgerin' the boy," said Jack, putting his arm protectively around Red Hawk's shoulder. "Let's head up to the Bear clan longhouse an' git us some supper."

"Yes, we have turtle soup!"

"That should make Will happy," chortled Hawkins. "O' course, now that Bright Star's nursin' 'im, he won't care what he eats."

"And that get them talking," added Jack's wife with a hopeful smile, "to work things out."

"What he really needs is fer Bright Star to turn back on his love supply. That'd heal him mighty quick!"

"I mention it to her," promised Little Mink just before they entered the longhouse door.

"Advice should help if come from another woman."

Jack and his family made their way through the smoky interior until they reached Sparrow's hearth. The clan mother greeted them warmly as she ladled out bowls of savory soup. Will was lying on a nearby sleeping platform with a peaceful expression wreathed on his face. Bright Star was patiently feeding him with the same wooden spoon she had used to drive him from the longhouse just a few months before.

After Hawkins wolfed down three servings of soup, he thanked his hostess, emitted a loud yawn, and crawled off to bed. He would have fallen instantly asleep if Little Mink hadn't tagged along to smother him with kisses. As they snuggled together, she took Jack's hand and held it against her belly. "Feel that?" she asked. "I have gift for you, too."

Hawkins stroked his wife's smooth stomach and, for the first time, noticed the prominent bulge growing there. He also felt a faint thump coming from inside. When he raised his eyebrows in concern, Little Mink said, "It's your son. By way he kick, him be fast runner like you."

Jack kissed his wife on the cheek and held her tight. "I helped the soldiers burn Kit-Han-Ne," he mumbled at last. "That's how Will got shot an' Red Hawk become an orphan. Soon, that whole country will be safe ag'in, so we should think about movin' back."

"It be nice to go home," agreed Little Mink. "And have own place."

"We's gonna need it," joshed Hawkins, "'cause afore long our youngins is gonna overrun this clan house."

"But what will you do? You not white farmer."

"Go back to trappin' a valley teemin' with beaver that Mac an' me found. Our hut's still there, but I reckon it's too small fer our family. Maybe we could build us a proper cabin. Maybe Will an' Bright Star would come along if we help 'em git back together."

"Having man who stay close to home is what Bright Star want."

"Then, this could work fer them," Jack said.

"How about Gathering Flowers and Alex?"

"Sure! Can't fergit them. Mac fought a terrible battle in Scotland that still haunts him, so I reckon a peaceful place is jess what he needs. I seen some bad things, myself, but bein' with you chases them nightmares away."

"Well, go to sleep, husband, and I'll love you in your dreams, too. Tomorrow, we talk more about valley where beaver grow thicker than ferns in forest."

POSTSCRIPT

After the burning of Kit-Han-Ne, the fierce warriors of the Lenni Lenape nation suspended their war with the English. The death of Captain Jacobs and fifty of his Wolf clan brethren convinced the Delaware to move west of Fort Duquesne for their own protection. There, they settled in the villages of Logstown, Sauconk, King Beaver's Town (Beaver Falls), and Kuskuskies (New Castle). They remained neutral for the rest of the French and Indian War.

BIBLIOGRAPHY

Axtell, James. <u>The European and the Indian: Essays in the Ethnohistory of Colonial North America</u>. Oxford: Oxford University Press, 1981.

Anderson, Fred. <u>The War That Made America</u>. New York: Viking Penguin, 2005.

<u>Ben Bowie and His Mountain Men</u>. New York: Dell Publishing Company, Feb.-April 1958.

"Bison," <u>Compton's Encyclopedia</u>, Vol. 3 (1984), pp. 285-286.

Borneman, Walter R. <u>The French & Indian War: Deciding the Fate of North America</u>. New York: Harper Collins Publisher, 2006.

Bruchac, Joseph. "A Mohawk Village in 1491: Otstungo," <u>National Geographic</u>, October 1991, pp. 68-82.

"Cycles," <http://www.olivetreegenealogy.com/moh/cycle.shtml> (31 October 2009).

Cho, Joon and Rohan Krishnan, "How the Iroquois Hunted," <http://www.oppapers.com/essays/Iroquois-Hunted/107694> (31 October 2009).

Doane, Nancy Locke. <u>Indian Doctor</u>. Charlotte, NC: Aerial Photographic Service, Inc.

"Figure-4 Deadfall," <http://www.wildwoodsurvival.com/survival/traps/fingure4.html> (28 October 2009).

Frazier, Jeffery R. <u>Pennsylvania Fireside Tales</u>. State College, PA: Jostens Commercial Publications, 1996.

Garbino, William. Along the Allegheny. Midway, PA: Midway Publishing, 2005.

"Iroquois Book of Rites Chapter VI: The Laws of the League," <http://www.sacredtexts.com/nam/iro/br/br07.htm> (1 November 2009).

"Iroquois Customs," <http://www.accessgenealogy.com/native/legends/customs.htm> (1 November 2009).

Karpovage, Michael. Crown of Serpents. Jonesboro, GA: Jacks River Communications, 2009.

Keene, Michael, "Three Mysteries Solved by Seneca Archaeological Findings," <http://ezinearticles.com/?Three-Mysteries-Solved-by-Seneca-Archae...> (1 November 2009).

Johnson, Michael. Tribes of the Iroquois Confedercy. Oxford, UK: Osprey Publishing, 2003.

McCafferty, Keith. "Primitive Survival Skills," Field & Stream, February 2006, pp.49-59.

McIlnay, Dennis P. Juniata, River of Sorrows. Hollidaysburg, PA: Seven Oaks Press, 2008.

Morgan, Lewis Henry and Herbert Marshall Lloyd. League of the Ho-De-No-Sau-Nee or Iroquois. New York: Dodd, Mead and Company, 1904.

Morgan, Robert. Boone A Biography. Chapel Hill, NC: Algonquin Books, 2007.

"Native American Religions in Early America," <http://nationalhumanitiescenter.org/tserve/eighteen/ekeyinfo/natrel.htm> (1 November 2009).

"Native American Survival: Fishing," <http://lakeland schools.org/It/NewYorkVM/nasurvfish.htm> (18 February 2008).

Oswalt, Wendell H. This Land Was Theirs. Boston: McGraw-Hill, 2002.

Pennsylvania: A History. Ed. George P. Donehoo. 4 vols. New York: Lewis Historical Publishing Co., Inc., 1926.

"Rangers in Colonial and Revolutionary America," <http://www.history.army.mil/documents/RevWar/revra.htm> (30 September 2009).

Richmond, Betty H. Young George Washington: Frontier Spy. Cochranton, PA: Specialty Group Printing of Crawford County, 2003.

Robertson, William P. and David Rimer. Ambush in the Alleghenies. Conshohocken, PA: Infinity Publishing, 2008.

Rogers, Timothy J. "Checkers,"<http://www.darkfish.com/checkers/Checkers.html> (23 October 2009).

Sipe, C. Hale. The Indian Chiefs of Pennsylvania. Lewisburg, PA: Wennawoods Publishing, 2004.

_____. The Indian Wars of Pennsylvania. Lewisburg, PA: Wennawoods Publishing, 2006.

Smail, Larry A. The Attack of Kit-Han-Ne Kittaning, Pennsylvania September 8, 1756. Chicora, PA: Mechling Bookbindery, 2006.

Waldman, Carl. Atlas of the North American Indian. New York: Checkmark Books, 2000.

War for Empire in Western Pennsylvania. Fort
    Ligonier Association, 1993.

Way, Frederick, Jr. The Allegheny. New York: Farrar
    & Rinehart, 1942.

Wellman, Paul I. Indian Wars and Warriors East.
    Cambridge, MA: The Riverside Press, 1959.

Marc Jackson as a Mohawk brave
(These Iroquois sided with British)

AUTHOR PROFILE: WILLIAM P. ROBERTSON

William P. Robertson was born and raised in the wilds of Pennsylvania and has been an avid woodsman since his youth. He first read exploits of the Eastern mountain men in the Ben Bowie comic books of the late 1950's. Soon, Bill was devouring all the Indian and pioneer biographies he found at Lincoln Elementary School in Bradford, PA. Some of his favorite tales were of Dan Morgan, Davy Crockett, and Black Hawk, the Sac chief. He also begged his parents to buy him Paul I. Wellman's wonderful book, <u>Indian Wars and Warriors East</u>. These stories, along with Bill's own hunting and fishing adventures, served as the inspiration for <u>Attack in the Alleghenies</u>. The author now hopes to have more fun as a French and Indian War reenactor. Below, he is dressed as a woodsman of the 1750's. And, yes, Bill did wear a coonskin cap when he was a lad.

AUTHOR PROFILE: DAVID RIMER

Currently retired, David Rimer taught speech and English for thirty-four years at Bradford Area High School in Bradford, PA. He received his BS degree from Clarion University, an MEd from Edinboro University, and further graduate credits from St. Bonaventure, Gannon, and East Stroudsburg Universities. David and his wife, Marcia, live in Bradford, PA. They have one daughter, Stephanie, who is a public school librarian. Mr. Rimer has edited several books for Robyl Press and is a published mystery author. He began collaborating with William P. Robertson in 1989 and co-wrote the seven novel Bucktail series about the famous Civil War sharpshooters, the 42nd Pennsylvania Volunteers. Robertson and Rimer's book, <u>The Bucktails at the Devil's Den</u> was a finalist in the Best Books 2007 Awards sponsored by USABookNews.com.

ALSO FROM INFINITY PUBLISHING

Ambush in the Alleghenies begins the adventures of Lightnin' Jack Hawkins, Alexander MacDonald, Will Big Cat Cutler, and Bearbite Bob Winslow, four freewheeling mountain men struggling to survive the primordial wilderness of colonial Pennsylvania. Dangers lurked everywhere there in the form of ferocious cougars, scalp-stealing savages, and white water rivers of immense fury. The woodsmen's worst nemesis, though, was Bold Wolf, the vicious Ottawa chief who brutally murdered Cutler's father and wanted to kill all the English like one pigeon. The trappers cross paths often with George Washington, too. They aid the young officer as he returns from spying on the French and then serve under him at Fort Necessity and at Braddock's Defeat. For ordering info, visit http://bucktailsandbroomsticks.com.

THE BUCKTAIL NOVEL SERIES

William P. Robertson and David Rimer have also collaborated on a seven-novel series about the famous Civil War rifle regiment—the Bucktails. Acting as skirmishers for the Union, these Pennsylvania sharpshooters were the equivalent of today's Army Rangers. The series traces the adventures of two frontier lads who stand the test of fire at Dranesville, Antietam, Gettysburg, and the Wilderness. Also detailed are the brutal marches, lousy rations, inept generals, and fearful diseases that made survival a true test of courage for these young riflemen. For more information about the books, visit Robertson's website at http://bucktailsandbroomsticks.com. The first four novels were published by White Mane, while Infinity Publishing produced the last three.

GLOSSARY

Alleghenies—Mountainous wilderness that stretches across western end of present-day Pennsylvania.

Black Fish—An Indian gambling game that uses a turtle shell to rattle game pieces that are made out of flat stones and fish-shaped stones painted black on one side.

Deadfall Trap—A trap so constructed that a log or other heavy weight falls on an animal to squash, kill, or disable it. It is set along trails or outside burrows where a passing animal can brush against the trigger.

Flintlock—Muzzle loading black powder firearm that employs a hammer holding a flint. When trigger is squeezed, cocked hammer falls, strikes a frizzen, and creates a spark that ignites priming powder poured in the pan.

Fort Duquesne—Built by the French at present-day Pittsburgh, Pennsylvania, to control traffic on the Allegheny, Monongahela, and Ohio Rivers.

Fort Granville—Pennsylvania fort burned by Captain Jacobs and Chevalier Villiers. Its destruction resulted in the attack on Kit-Han-Ne.

Gauntlet—Double file of Indians facing each other and armed with clubs, switches, and axes with which to strike a captive who is forced to run between them.

Kit-Han-Ne—Indian village located at present-day Kittanning, Pennsylvania. The Delaware and Shawnee tribes used this town as a base from which to attack the frontiers of Pennsylvania, Maryland, and Virginia.

Longhouse—House over a hundred feet in length made of a wooden frame and covered with elm bark. This was main dwelling used by Iroquois tribe.

Militien—French Canadian colonial troops or militia that assisted in the Indian raids of Western Pennsylvania. Usually only served during summer months and returned home in winter.

Pennsylvania Long Rifle—Rifled flintlock musket used by the hunters and trappers of the Alleghenies. Was accurate up to 300 yards.

Possibles Bag—Bag with a shoulder strap used by hunters to carry their shooting supplies, trail food, and personal items.

Quakers—William Penn founded Pennsylvania as a haven for other members of his religion—the Quakers. Quakers controlled the Provincial Council in 1756. They did not believe in war, so were slow to help settlers under attack by the Delaware.

Ranger—Full-time soldier hired by colonial governments to reconnoiter the frontier and warn settlers of impending Indian raids. Also led offensive strikes against Indian villages deep in hostile territory. A ranger was an experienced woodsman taught to fight hand-to-hand in all types of weather and terrain.

Sachem—An Indian chief.

Scalp—War trophy taken by Indians who cut the hair from the crown of an enemy's head as proof of their kill. Showed warriors' power and bravery.

Scalp Lock—Strip of hair on the crown of the otherwise shaved head of an Indian warrior. Also known as Mohawk Haircut.

CHARACTERS

Lightnin' Jack Hawkins—Eastern mountain man and fur trapper known for his quickness. Named Swift Lightning by the Delaware tribe.

Alexander MacDonald—Hawkins' Scottish partner known for his hatred of the British and his pacifism. His friends called him "Mac."

Will Cutler—Young trapper nicknamed "Big Cat." He's skilled with all kinds of weapons. A bad marriage soured him on life.

Bearbite Bob Winslow—An old mountain man known for his womanizing, courage, and trapping abilities.

Bear Woman—Bearbite Bob's Iroquois wife.

Bright Star—The cold Iroquois princess married to Will Cutler.

Dark Thunder—A stern Iroquois sachem and father of Bright Star.

Sparrow—Bright Star's mother. She was known for her strength of character.

Gathering Flowers—MacDonald's Iroquois wife.

Shingas—Delaware chief who led raids on Western Pennsylvania. Although small in stature, was known for his courage and savage prowess.

Captain Jacobs—Stout Delaware war chief named after a German farmer from Cumberland County who resembled him.

Willow—Captain Jacobs' kindly wife. She was killed with her husband at Kit-Han-Ne.

Young Jacobs—Bullying son of Captain Jacobs. Was said to be seven feet tall.

Red Hawk—Captain Jacobs' youngest son who befriended Jack Hawkins.

King Beaver—Shingas' brother who also led war parties to Pennsylvania settlements.

John Hickman—Another Delaware chief who dwelt at Kit-Han-Ne.

Little Mink—Jack Hawkins' beautiful Delaware wife. She believed the Great Spirit brought Jack to her.

Many Shots—Young brave who captured Mary Martin at Big Cove to be his bride.

Long Arrow—A teenage friend of Young Jacobs who also hated Jack Hawkins.

Rushing Bear—Another of Young Jacobs' savage pals.

Rupert Miller—A villainous rum trader who captured Hawkins and took him to Kit-Han-Ne.

Randall Miller—Rupert's equally evil brother.

Lieutenant Colonel John Armstrong—Led the Pennsylvania army that destroyed Kit-Han-Ne.

Lieutenant Edward Armstrong—Younger brother of John Armstrong. He was killed at the burning of Fort Granville after displaying great bravery.

Captain Edward Ward—Was the commanding officer of Fort Granville and also led a company of men against Kit-Han-Ne.

Chevalier Louis Coulon de Villiers—French officer who won the Battle of Fort Necessity and later burned Fort Granville.

John Baker—After escaping from Kit-Han-Ne, he drew a map of the village for Colonel Armstrong.

Thomas Burke—An old trader who acted as an advanced scout during the Kittanning raid.

James Chalmers—Another old scout and friend of Burke.

John Ferguson—Set Captain Jacob's house on fire during the Kittanning raid. His heroics resulted in the chief's death.

Robert Stray Wolf, Delaware reenactor